HORNET

BOOK DESCRIPTION

A citizen reporter must stop hummingbird-sized hornets from destroying a resort town before the government unleashes its own devious scheme to eliminate them.

When a swarm of murder hornets invades a Lake Michigan resort town, citizen reporter Pacie Rose and her sidekick cousin struggle to find what is causing mutant stinging wasps, now grown to the size of hummingbirds, from attacking the residents of Black Water, while also working against an aggressive, and unwelcome, secret government plot that could do as much if not more harm to the residents as the killer hornets in this natural horror.

ConnieMyres.com

HORNET

Pacie Rose Mysteries, #2

ConnieMyres.com
FEATHER AND FERMION PUBLISHING

Connie Myres

Feather and Fermion Publishing

Hornet / Connie Myres

ISBN: 978-1-957819-12-9 (e-book)
ISBN: 978-1-957819-13-6 (hardcover)
ISBN: 978-1-957819-14-3 (paperback)

DEDICATION

*To my family, my friends, and those who have supported me
though my journey as an author. I appreciate you.*

CONTENTS

PART I:

Who Let the Bees Out?

1

Going Postal

Such true hornets are big, predatory, colony-forming wasps. They belong to the genus Vespa. None are native to North or South America. Most are native to Asia. They need meat to feed their young. That contrasts with honeybees, which collect plant pollen as protein. Another difference is that a honeybee dies after its single-use stinger rips out of its body. Hornets can sting over and over.

—Science News

* * *

When she reached the battered black metal mailbox, Lucille Owens slammed her edematous foot down on the mail truck's brake. A cloud of early June dust rolled in billows through the large, open window, settling on the already filthy interior. With the experience of a Frisbee tossing champion, she propelled the mail into the dented box with a flip of the wrist. She closed the warped door with a twist, causing it to fall back open. That is where she left it, as she pushed down hard on the gas pedal. The tires flung gravel, pelting a nearby garbage can.

"I hate this job," Lucille said, slamming on the brakes as she approached the next mailbox, causing a variety of odd-shaped boxes and packages in the back of the truck to shift. "There has to be some law against changing work schedules at the last minute. The union stewards are so worthless."

Lucille took a lit cigarette from the red plastic ashtray sitting on the dash, gulped a long draft of smoke, and then secured the cancer stick back into a notch of the overflowing receptacle. She coughed, almost vomiting, as she flung shiny ads into the box, then pulled onto the next driveway and drove up to the farmhouse. The truck's brakes squealed like an alarm alerting the homeowners to come and get their box from hell, but no one came out the door. The only thing that stirred was Sweet Pea, a Rottweiler that barked at her every time she had to deliver packages to the farm. Fortunately, a chain kept the dog contained near his doghouse. Whenever she had to get out of the truck and take something to the house, she worried the ferocious dog would break free from its chain and attack her. She was sure today would be the day.

When Lucille first began delivering to the residence, she tried talking to Sweet Pea, but it never calmed the dog's aggressiveness. Even using its name, hand-painted with light blue paint in fancy cursive above its cottage garden doghouse, did nothing to help the situation. She had thought about buying a can of Mace to carry on her in case she needed to spray the unruly creature, but never got around to it. Besides, if things got so bad that Macing good ol' Sweet Pea was necessary, she would plain and simply not deliver packages to the house if they did not fit in the mailbox. And who named it Sweet Pea, anyway? It should be called Killer, Fang, or Cujo, not given the name of a delicate flower.

Lucille was angry when she climbed out of the truck. Not only because of the schedule change that was ruining the wedding that she wanted to attend, but because there were so many packages to deliver. Everyone was making online purchases, and each one added time and effort to her already rushed workday.

Lucille walked to the back of the truck and rolled up the door. She climbed inside, stepping on some of the smaller packages piled on the floor.

"Where are you?" Lucille said as she fumbled through the scattered parcels. She turned the bigger boxes side to side so that she could read their address. "How'd you get way up there? I thought I put you by the door."

Lucille knew why. All the sudden moves made by the truck caused packages to shift and fall over and onto each other. This was not new. The truck was always a cluttered mess, but it was not totally her fault. It was the fault of the manager, who was always making her take extra packages from the new carriers who were slow and had not yet mastered the routes.

With the bulky box now found, she flipped it over until the end of it was sticking out the back of the truck.

"What are people ordering, barbells? This has to weigh over seventy pounds."

As Lucille tugged the maximum-weight box through the cargo compartment, a smaller package dragged along with it until falling to the ground. She picked up the square white cardboard package and noticed that it was from the government and marked LIVE QUEEN BEES. She heard a raspy humming sound coming through the wire mesh vents on two sides of the box and felt movement, as if there were mice inside and not bees.

"Oh, yeah, you're my bee package." Lucille sat it on the truck's step bumper, then continued wiggling the awkward box until it was out of the truck and standing on end beside her.

"Why don't they pack these things in boxes with handles? It's like moving every mattress I've ever owned. Ridiculous."

Lucille pulled down the truck's door and gripped the box that towered over her head. She tilted it side to side until she had walked it into the open garage door, where she leaned it against the wall next to a grass-clipping-covered lawnmower.

The canine on the other side of the garage was thrusting its body weight against the dog chain's metal links. Sweet Pea snarled, bearing its saliva-dripping teeth. Lucille was afraid to move for a moment, fearing that it would trigger the dog to fight against the chain even harder and detach from the already compromised stake that was loosening its anchor to the ground.

A cracking sound came from the dog's tether, causing Lucille to jump and break free from the frozen position that she was in. She made a mad dash back to the truck as Sweet

Pea ran after her with the chain dragging behind him. Lucille closed the driver's door just as the dog pounced on the truck, making it rock. Like the Duke boys, she sped down the driveway, leaving Sweet Pea barking after her.

Lucille tore onto the road, pulling in front of an approaching red semi-truck with a loaded flatbed trailer. The driver blew the air horn, not letting up for even a moment. The only good thing about the obnoxious trucker was that he also scared Sweet Pea, causing the beast to return to his doghouse.

"Pass me, you jerk," Lucille yelled, even though she knew there was no room for the truck to get around her safely because of the road's curves, hills, and oncoming traffic. Even when she pulled onto the road's shoulder to deliver mail, he stayed on her butt.

"Can this damned day get any worse?" Lucille said, complaining to the mirror as she watched the eighteen-wheeler tailgate. She could hear him yelling something out of his window, but she could not make out what he was saying. "What does he expect me to do, drive in the ditch so he can pass? What a nutcase."

Her route turned onto another road. Lucille quickly swung the mail truck out of the trucker's path, hoping he was not going her way. He was not. However, she saw the small package she had forgotten about fly off her bumper and into the semi's path, where the trailer's tires ripped it to shreds. Pieces of paper and whatever else was inside the box flew into the air and scattered along the roadside.

"Oops, I didn't mean to do that. But I am surprised it stayed on my bumper this long. There's no sense going back for it; there's nothing left." Lucille shrugged. "Hopefully, the bees survived."

* * *

The Asian giant hornet poked its orange head out from under a piece of the shredded cardboard box. She wiggled her damaged brown antennae, touching the tattered debris from which it emerged. The two sensory organs on her head assessed the situation by smelling, tasting, and listening to the foreign surroundings. With her faithful eight attendants at her side, she took flight to find the perfect spot for a new nest in which to form a colony.

2

Two Months Later

Pacie Rose dipped a finger into the homemade hummingbird food she had made in a small pot on the kitchen stove. It was cool enough to fill the feeder she had just bought. "I know it's August and I should've done this earlier, but there are at least a couple of months left before the hummingbirds migrate south."

"Next year you can put it out in May," her cousin and sidekick Irma Foster said as she turned over the package surrounding the red plastic feeder and read, "Bee resistant. The unique dome shape of the feeder lid creates a space between the feeding port opening and the nectar that is held in the base dish. A hummingbird's tongue is twice the length of the bird's bill, allowing it to easily reach down into the bottom of the dish to the sweet nectar. Bees and wasps have much shorter tongues and cannot reach the liquid. Though bees and wasps may still initially be attracted to the feeder, they will eventually lose interest once they find they cannot reach the food."

"Wow, hummingbirds have tongues that long!" Pacie said, stirring the nectar in the pot to make sure the sugar had dissolved.

"Their tongues are even forked," Irma said, removing the feeder from the package. "But it's a good thing that it doesn't attract bees since you're allergic to them."

"No doubt," Pacie said as she filled the feeder with the sugar water. "Let's put it on one of the little parlor windows so that I can see it while I'm watching TV."

"That's about the best place since you and Patrick took out the only windows in the study when you added the kitchen and bathroom, along with the garage. I think that was a design flaw," Irma said as she and Mr. Dibble, a muscular Staffordshire terrier, followed Pacie outside.

"I hear you, but there is some light that filters into the study from other rooms, like the butler's pantry. We didn't want to destroy too much of the mansion's historical charm. We wanted to keep most of its Palladium style as possible. The original kitchen wasn't even attached to the house—I didn't want to go to another building just to make a sandwich." Pacie looked back at Irma and smiled. "Besides, when I'm writing in the study, I'm supposed to be working, not staring out the window and procrastinating . . . one of my bad habits."

As they walked outside, a pleasant Lake Michigan breeze blew along the bluff and through the pillared, two-story piazza that stretched the length of the mansion.

Mr. Dibble walked onto the grass and sniffed along the edge of the piazza where it met the lawn while Pacie pressed the feeder's suction cups against the glass of the parlor window.

"I think you need to put it down a bit so that you can see the top of it and the hummingbirds better," Irma said.

"Makes sense," Pacie said, putting it on a lower pane of glass.

Irma looked at Mr. Dibble, who was digging in the dirt by the porch. "Mr. Dibble, stop that."

"He must've found something interesting," Pacie said, pressing again on the suction cups to ensure the feeder was secured to the window.

Mr. Dibble did not listen as he kept throwing the sandy soil into the air behind him.

Irma walked up to the determined dog. "Mr. Dibble, you're making a hole in Pacie's yard."

Pacie joined Irma and the busy dog to see what was so important to him. "I don't see anything."

Irma pulled gently on Mr. Dibble's leash to refocus his attention, but he continued moving the soil with his paws as if a buried treasure were only one more scoop of soil away. "Stop digging in Pacie's yard and go do something else."

Mr. Dibble looked up at Irma, and with a knowing glance—between pooch and owner—stopped digging. With a snort, he continued to sniff along the foundation.

Irma used the side of her shoe to push the soil back into the hole. "Sorry about that."

"No biggie," Pacie said. "Oh, by the way, I'm going to get Johnny's new boat out of storage for him so that we can go fishing. You can come along with us if you want."

"I didn't know you fished. Patrick didn't fish, did he?"

"Not really. When Patrick was alive, we would just go for boat rides. I haven't done much fishing since I was a kid catching bass and bluegill from our little pond." Pacie smiled at the memory of her mom cleaning the fish that tasted like mud. "I'm actually more interested in getting out on the water this summer than I am in catching Chinook, lake trout, or whatever Johnny said was good to catch this time of year."

Irma shrugged. "I don't want to be a fifth wheel."

"You won't be," Pacie said. "It's not a special occasion, just something to do while the weather's warm. Mr. Dibble can come, too."

"I do need to get out of my apartment," Irma said, looking out over the Great Lake. "When are you doing this?"

"I don't know, sometime soon. I'm going to the marina this afternoon and have them get the boat out of storage and dock it."

"He bought an old yacht, didn't he?" Irma asked.

"Old is right. He got a great deal on it. It's one of those motor sailboats. This will be the first time he's taken it out, and I'm not so sure I trust his sailing abilities."

Irma laughed. "He should take lessons."

"I doubt he'll do that, so make sure you're wearing a life jacket if you decide to come with us. And it wouldn't hurt to bring an oar; we might end up rowing to shore." Pacie grinned and shook her head. "Want to go with me to the marina this afternoon? We can stop and get something to eat."

Using her foot, Irma packed down the dirt she had pushed into the hole. "Sure, I'll ride with you."

Pacie turned to walk back inside the house when she heard a buzzing sound. "I hear a hummingbird already."

"Uh," Irma paused and then said, "you'd better look at this."

Pacie looked back at the feeder and saw a large hornet. "Oh my god. That's not a hummingbird, that's a bee."

"Not a bee, a big wasp," Irma said, stepping back. "It's almost as big as a hummingbird. It has to be a queen, but this is just plain not normal."

On the plastic body of the feeder, a black and orange banded hornet with an orange head was probing the ports, trying to gain access to the nectar.

Keeping her distance, Pacie said, "Is that one of those murder hornets? I thought they had only invaded Washington State."

"I don't know if it is or not," Irma said, "but whatever it is, we should call someone. It has to be some kind of mutation."

"I think the State of Michigan has a honeybee protection plan that we could call." Pacie backed toward the door, not wanting to lose sight of the giant wasp. "You'd better grab Mr. Dibble and get him inside because if there's one of those things around, there's probably more."

"I wouldn't be surprised if that monster killed every honeybee it came across," Irma said as she looked around for Mr. Dibble. She whistled for him to come to her. "I wonder where it came from, because something like that is certainly not native to Black Water. It's an invasive species of some kind."

"I think we have another mystery to solve—giant wasps attack Black Water," Pacie said. "I'll bet it's one of those Asian giant hornets."

Mister Dibble ran up to Irma. "Murder hornets are big, but don't get that big, not even the queens. It must be something else. It reminds me of those penguins in South Africa that were killed by bees. I guess Cape honeybees stung them around the eyes and flippers where they don't have many feathers."

"I saw that, too. The swarm killed sixty of those poor penguins, and they were an endangered species. They might have gotten too close to a hive," Pacie said as she opened the door. "Whatever kind of wasp that is on the feeder, we need to figure out why it's here and how to get rid of it. Because if it is a murder hornet or something like it, many people could die."

The three of them rushed inside and into the parlor.

"You should take the feeder down," Irma said. She kept her distance from the window as if the wasp were about to break through the glass. "It'll attract more of them to the house."

"I don't know," Pacie said, inching closer to the window to get a better look at the unrelenting hornet. "I just might keep it there so that I can try to figure out what it is, maybe take some pictures."

"You may want to rethink that." Irma contorted her lips. "That just plain sounds crazy. But what I do know is that I want you to pick me up when we go to the marina later. I'm not so sure I want to come back here, especially since you're baiting murder hornets."

"It could be something different," Pacie said. "It could be harmless. That's what we need to figure out. I don't want to jump to conclusions and panic everyone in Black Water."

"Just promise me you'll keep your EpiPen handy," Irma said.

"So, are you with me on taking the case of the giant bees?" Pacie said.

"I'm with you. But what I don't like is that since I'm not allergic to bees, I'm going to have to be the one who has to get close to them."

"We'll have to track you down one of those beekeeper suits." Pacie smiled.

Irma rolled her eyes. "I guess I'm going to head home and see if there have been any other sightings around town and make a call to the DNR."

"Okay, I'll see you later."

As Irma and Mr. Dibble left, Pacie stood in front of the window watching the hornet that had not given up on trying to get to the sugar water. It surprised her that her movement behind the glass did not scare it off; it paid little attention to her. At least until it looked up from a perch, appearing to make eye contact with her.

"No way," Pacie said, watching its beady black eyes. One of its brown antennae was bent as if it had been damaged somehow. "I think it's really looking at me."

3

Road Rage

Pacie drove to downtown Black Water and parked in the parking lot behind Johnathon Armstrong's antique shop. She walked in the back door so that she could see Johnny before she and Irma left for the marina.

"Hey, good lookin'," Johnny said from his work area behind the counter. He sat down the screwdriver he was using to adjust the lid of a Renaissance-style box and wiped his hands on a shop rag as Pacie walked up to him.

"Hey, handsome."

Johnny stood and pulled her close to him. He planted a passionate kiss on her lips. "Are you going to get Six Feet Under out of storage today?"

"Six Feet Under?" Pacie raised an eyebrow. "Is that what you're calling your boat?"

"Sure. Why not?"

"It sounds so ominous. Like you're expecting it to end up on the floor of Lake Michigan."

Johnny gave her another kiss and sat down on the workbench stool, refocusing his attention on the ornamental box. "Lake Michigan doesn't have sharks, so there's nothing to worry about."

"I beg to differ. It's still an inland sea, meaning it's deep with lots of water." Pacie watched him manipulate the box's lid. "How about something nicer, like White Pearl?"

"I don't know," Johnny said, continuing to work the stubborn hinge. "Too feminine."

"No, it's not."

Johnny shrugged, then said, "Zombie Refuge."

Pacie laughed. "I kinda like it."

"Kinda? The way the world is these days, it could come in handy for just that reason."

"So, you're predicting the future now?"

Johnny looked up at Pacie, who was leaning against the bench with her arms crossed. He put a hand on her hip. "This has to be what it's like to name a kid."

Pacie nodded and smiled. Johnny had no children. He spent his bachelor life focusing on his business, Good Old Days Antique Shop. The store was his love and his baby. But now that he's grown older and with Pacie in his life, he mentioned to her they should get married. Even though it has been a while since her late husband was presumed drowned; without the body, she couldn't totally put him to rest.

"I haven't answered your question yet," Pacie said.

"Thanks for noticing," Johnny said, now working on the latch.

"Yeah, I'm going to be heading to the marina shortly. Irma's going with me."

"I can't wait for the two of us to get out on the water, far from the shore and away from prying eyes." He winked.

"Oh." Pacie looked down and then back up, avoiding eye contact. "I invited Irma to go with us."

Johnny sighed. "Why am I not surprised? You two are attached at the hip."

"I'm sorry. I didn't realize you had other *things* in mind." Pacie winked back. "I'll make it up to you."

"You'd better, Pacie Rose. I already don't get to see you enough as it is."

"I know."

"There, it's fixed," Johnny said, lifting and lowering the lid on the box.

The shop's front door jingled. Two middle-aged women walked inside. Dressed in paint-stained jeans and T-shirts, they looked like they were on the hunt for a new project to work on.

"Well, Irma's waiting for me. I'd better get going."

Johnny kissed her again. "I'll talk to you later."

While Johnny greeted the potential customers, Pacie walked through the backdoor that led to the elevator and staircase. Johnny's old handwritten note stating that the old Otis Elevator was out of order still covered the lift's call station. It was just as well because she didn't trust the old thing, anyway. It was so old that the inner door of the cab was a sliding scissor door. She had ridden in it up to Johnny's apartment only once. It clinked, clanked, and felt so unsteady that she refused to ride it again. Johnny had it inspected, and repairs were made, but he never removed the sign. She guessed he didn't trust the old thing either.

She climbed the creaking steps to Irma's apartment, the only one on the second floor. A seashell wreath, adorned with an assortment of shells, starfish, and driftwood, hung on the dark wooden door. She gave a courtesy knock and walked inside.

"Hi, Pacie. I'm almost ready," Irma said, walking out of the bedroom, adjusting the elastic on the waist of her pants.

"Don't rush; we've got time to get there before they close."

Irma went into the bathroom while Mr. Dibble raised his head from where he was sleeping on the couch and looked at Pacie.

"How are you today, Mr. Dibble," Pacie said, patting him on top of his head.

Mr. Dibble jumped off the couch and went to his water bowl. Pacie walked over to Irma's desk, where a book of Common Michigan Bees and a notepad of handwritten notes lay on the surface next to her laptop. A half-cup of coffee—probably cold—sat near the computer mouse in a mug with Mr. Dibble's, so ugly it's cute, face on it.

Mr. Dibble laid down on the front door rug, waiting for the car ride he knew was on the way.

Irma came out of the bathroom smelling of hairspray. "I'm ready."

Mr. Dibble stood up, preparing to dart out the door the moment it opened.

The cuckoo call from the pendulum wall clock announced the 2 o'clock hour. Pacie watched the bird pop out of a door on the chalet-style cuckoo clock, then turned toward Irma. "Are you hungry?"

"I'm starved," Irma said, slipping her cellphone into her fanny pack.

"Did you do any research on big bees?"

"I did. Looks like we're not the only ones who have spotted the abnormal wasps." Irma unhooked her keys from the backpack sitting next to her desk. "I called Andy at the paper and Janet at the station. They both have had a couple of sightings reported, but no injuries."

"Other than the sightings themselves, did anyone report being stung?"

"No, just the sightings. One person saw a giant wasp while he was mowing the lawn; it was attacking the mower. It scared him so much that he raced into the house, leaving the mower in the middle of the yard with its engine still running. He thought the noise was making the wasp aggressive."

"It probably was. A while back, I remember my dad saying that a snake attacked the rider while he was mowing around the pond."

"That's weird." Irma picked up her backpack and walked toward the door. "The guy also said it circled him and looked as though it was going to attack him."

"That sounds dangerous. Other people in town are probably experiencing the same thing."

"I posted all this on our website."

"If we see any of those hornets while we're out today, I'll call pest control and see what we can do to get rid of them."

"Give Oscar a call at Oscar's Vermin Control. He's a little scattered brained, but he does a good job." Irma sat her backpack and keys on the kitchen counter and began rummaging underneath the sink. "I used him at my old house to get rid of some pesky ants—those little ones that gang up on a piece of dropped food. They look like a blurry pile of dirt, at least when I don't have my glasses on."

Pacie heard containers falling over. She watched as Irma sat a jug of bleach on the floor next to her foot, apparently to further her search deeper into the dark space. "What are you doing?"

"I'm looking for a spray bottle."

"Why?" Irma pulled out a plastic window cleaner bottle. "I read that spraying wasps with water and dish soap might stop them from attacking."

"If they're that close, it might be time to run." Pacie leaned on the counter. "It might be easier, and work better, if we stop at the store and get a can of wasp killer."

Irma unscrewed the spray mechanism and added water to the almost empty bottle. Two good squirts of dish soap finished off the poison. "I have no idea if this works, but it's better safe than sorry."

"So, spray and then run might save the day."

"I don't know about running. Murder Hornets—if that's what they are—can fly around twenty-five miles per hour, around the same as the fastest human." Irma closed the nozzle and put it into the backpack. "*Now* I'm ready."

"Unfortunately, I don't think we're close to being the fastest humans. Not even when I was younger—decades ago—and ran high school track." Pacie opened the door and Mr. Dibble shot out, as expected. "I think we'd lose that race."

"Mr. Dibble would win," Irma said, following Pacie out the apartment door.

They left the building, nervously looking around for any bees as they climbed into Pacie's silver SUV. Irma locked her door.

"You do realize bees can't break into cars. Right?" Pacie laughed.

Irma ignored her, opting instead to stare at the insect-attracting dumpster.

Pacie backed out of the parking spot. "I think we're being a little paranoid."

"Maybe," Irma said, looking back at Mr. Dibble who was sitting up in the middle of the backseat as if a child. "I've got a bad feeling about this. The hornet we saw was abnormally huge, after all."

Pacie drove onto the street. "Where do you want to eat when we're done at the marina?"

Irma thought a moment. She took a cigarette and lighter from her fanny pack and held them for Pacie to see. "Mind if I smoke?"

"When are you giving up those things? You know they're no good for you."

Irma lit the cigarette and took a drag. She coughed, then said in a raspy voice. "Ya gotta die of something."

Pacie shook her head. "True, but I'd rather die of old age."

Irma lowered her window partway as Pacie pulled up to a stop sign. A scream from Irma and the motion of Mr. Dibble jumping to the front seat startled Pacie, causing her to slam on the brakes. "Get it out! Get it out!" Irma screamed.

That's when Pacie saw it—the giant hornet flying along the dash of the car. Her foot pressed full down on the gas pedal as she moved her body to get away from it and Mr. Dibble, who kept trying to catch it with his teeth. The powerful pit bull pushed against Pacie's arms—his focus only on the bee—causing her to swerve the SUV into the path of a semi-tractor-trailer truck.

The truck blasted its air horn as it braked; its tires spewed smoke as the cab rocked.

Pacie turned the steering wheel back the other way, barely missing the red flatbed truck. She pulled into the nearest driveway and they all shot out of the car, including the bee that buzzed away.

"What the hell?" Pacie said, crossing her arms close to her body.

Irma grabbed Mr. Dibble's collar, keeping him from chasing after the hornet.

Pacie's hands shook from the narrow escape with the truck and the hornet. "Are you all right?"

Irma was gasping for air as if she had just run a mile. "I think so. How about you? You weren't stung, were you?"

"No, thank God."

Irma inspected Mr. Dibble's mouth. "Doesn't look like Mr. Dibble got stung from biting at the hornet. I think we're all okay."

The air smelled of burned rubber as the trucker ran up to them. "Are you two broads crazy? What's up with this town? Doesn't anyone know how to drive around here? I could've killed you. Lucky for you, I wasn't loaded. Do you know how long it takes for a truck to stop? What's your damned hurry—on your way to the beauty parlor?"

Pacie looked at the pissed off trucker; a young guy dressed in dirty blue jeans and a gray tee shirt. She thought for a moment he was going to punch them by the way he was flexing his arm muscles. "I'm sorry, but a bee flew into the car and—

"I don't give a crap what you two old biddies' excuse is. Learn to drive." He stormed back to his truck.

Pacie watched him walk around the trailer, checking the tires and whatever else needed to be checked. The sign on the cab door said Greg Gumby Trucking.

Irma and Mr. Dibble climbed back into the car.

Pacie sighed and walked back to the open driver's door. "Are we sure there are no bees inside?"

"Yeah, there was only one, and it flew away. That hornet was as big as the one at the house." Irma puffed the cigarette she had managed not to drop. "That guy called us a couple of old biddies. Can you believe it?"

"What I do believe is that Black Water has a big problem." Pacie forcefully fastened her seat belt. "And I'm not an old biddy."

4

Black Bart

Pacie put the SUV in reverse, paused, then put it back into park.

"What are you doing? Are you too stressed to drive? I know I would be—if I could drive."

"I can see that." Pacie nodded. "But I just thought that we should see if we can find that bee. That way, we have evidence of what we're seeing. It's probably injured from Mr. Dibble biting it and could be on the ground someplace." Pacie looked down the driveway and saw a swing set in the home's backyard. She unhooked her seatbelt. "Besides, if it is injured, I don't want a little kid picking it up or stepping on it and getting stung."

Irma took a small glass baby food jar from her backpack and put her spent cigarette inside; she screwed the lid on tight. Then she took out Mr. Dibble's leash and opened her door. "If we do find it, I might be able to tell what kind of hornet it is or at least come close."

Pacie walked around to Irma, who had finished putting the dog on its leash. "We need something to put it in if we find it. Do you have anything in that bag of yours?"

"I believe so," Irma said, rummaging through the backpack as she had done underneath the kitchen sink. After a few mumbles, she pulled out a gallon-size plastic zippered bag. "This should be big enough."

Pacie looked at the freshly mowed lawn that surrounded the white clapboard bungalow. The aroma of the sweet smell of green caused her to draw in a full breath of air as if doing so would fill her soul with happiness. "Which way did it go?"

Irma pointed toward evergreen shrubs in front of the picture window, flanked on both sides with royal blue shutters. "I think it went that direction."

Mr. Dibble pulled on the leash as he sniffed the grass.

"Let's follow him," Pacie said. "But first I should let the homeowners know what we're doing so that they don't call the police on us."

"Doesn't look like anyone's home."

Pacie followed a sandstone path to the front door. She knocked, and no one answered. "Guess you're right."

Irma and Mr. Dibble were inspecting the front of the house as Pacie walked over to them. On the other side of the picture window sat a large black cat on the back of a couch, watching them.

Mr. Dibble grew restless in front of a rounded boxwood bush.

"Here," Irma said as she handed the leash to Pacie. "Keep him back so that I can look around."

Pacie took the loop handle of Mr. Dibble's leash and backed away while Irma separated the shrub branches, carefully looking for the giant hornet.

"I don't see it," Irma said as she continued her search.

Mr. Dibble kept tugging on the leash, wanting to get to the bush. Then a little striped chipmunk—with berries or a nut in its mouth—shot out from underneath it and scrambled to a nearby oak tree. With tremendous force, the dog's powerful body darted after the rodent, causing the leash to break free from Pacie's hand. She watched as Mr. Dibble tried to climb the tree after the furry little creature.

"I guess it wasn't the hornet he was after," Pacie said, rubbing her sore hand.

Irma kept exploring the front of the house while Pacie retrieved Mr. Dibble. They searched for a bit longer, then gave up.

"It must not have been injured that badly," Pacie said. "Let's just head to the marina and get Johnny's boat taken care of. I think they close at five."

The roar of the semi-truck's engine caught Pacie's attention. She watched as the driver flipped her off and drove away. "I'm glad he's gone."

"Don't pay any attention to him," Irma said as she opened the back door of the SUV. Mr. Dibble jumped inside, ready for another ride. "He's a punk."

Now back on the road, they crossed the double-leafed drawbridge over Inky River, drove past the maritime museum, then turned into Black Water Marina.

Pacie parked, and she and Irma got out. There were boats everywhere. From aluminum fish boats to luxurious yachts, all lined neatly on both land and water. A gentle breeze created a clinking melody as rigging pushed against masts. Gulls screeched and laughed in the distance.

Three blue-colored buildings surrounded the main parking area. The largest was marked as high and dry storage. The one on the other side of the lot was service and parts. And directly in front of them, the building had a sign above the door, painted in deep blue letters, that said Harbormaster and had an image of an anchor next to it.

"I guess that's where we need to go," Pacie said. "They've expanded the place since I was last here with Patrick."

They walked inside what seemed like a maritime truck stop. A service counter was in front of them, and the walls and shelves were stocked with various marine supplies that any level of boater might need, from navigation instruments to galley decor. A sit-down restaurant was at the back. Signage showed restrooms and showers. And an arrow pointed to a fish cleaning station.

At the service counter were an old man and a young woman. Pacie hesitated when she looked at the ancient guy; his name tag said Bart, Harbormaster. He reminded her of the fictional cartoon character Popeye. He had a squinty face, bulging forearms, and a white sailor cap—a dixie cup—on his head. Instead of a pipe, he held a toothpick in his mouth.

"How can I help you ladies?" said the gravelly-voiced Popeye lookalike. "I'm Bartholomew, but people call me Black Bart." He pointed to a framed painting on the wall.

The picture was of a man in his thirties, sitting in a chair with a pipe in his hand and a hat with feathers on his head. It could've been him in his youth when dressed up in costume as a pirate for a play or Halloween. Pacie was not sure what to say. "Is that you?"

Black Bart laughed. "Nah, that's my ancestor, the real Black Bart. A famous Welsh pirate from back in the day."

The young woman clad in summer clothes more suited to a tavern server cocked her head toward them. "He tells that story to all the new people. I told him he needs to get a DNA test, then I'll believe him." She turned back to the customer on the other side of the counter.

"Ah, don't pay attention to Tara," Black Bart said. His gaze moved to Irma, standing slightly to the back and side of Pacie. "Oh, such loveliness." He extended a hand toward Irma.

Pacie looked at the wrinkly, gray-haired Irma who was blushing as she put her dry-skinned hand into his. Having been called old biddies earlier, it was obvious that beauty was in the eye of the beholder.

"Nice to meet you." Irma's voice softened.

Black Bart held her hand an uncomfortably long time before finally releasing it. He kept his attention on Irma. "How may I help you?"

Irma cleared her throat. She gave a nod toward Pacie. "We're here to get Pacie's boyfriend's boat out of storage. I just came along for the ride."

"I can help you with that." Black Bart took a step to the computer. "Whose name is the vessel under?"

"Johnathon Armstrong," Pacie said.

Keyboard keys clicked. "Ah, here it is. A forty-one-foot sailing yacht. An oldie but goodie. I remember when Mr. Armstrong brought it in. We fixed damaged sails, a blocked toilet, a malfunctioning water maker, replaced the battery, and so forth. In other words, we made it seaworthy. What are Mr. Armstrong's plans?"

"He needs it serviced and put into a boat slip," Pacie said. "Johnny bought it last year and hasn't even had it out on the water yet. So, make sure the engine runs, the sails are good, and that there aren't any holes." Pacie laughed. "I'm not even sure he knows how to drive—I mean, sail it."

"No problem. We'd be happy to give Mr. Armstrong sailing instruction when he launches. Just let us know ahead of time and we'll have someone go out on the water with him." Black Bart took the toothpick out of his mouth. "We have a two-week sailing course if he's interested."

"I'll let him know."

With the toothpick back between his lips, he said, "We'll do a complete check on it and get back with Mr. Armstrong on any repairs that may be needed. I see there's not a name on the old gal. Is there anything you want to put here? We have a special going on for hand-painted boat names."

Pacie thought of her earlier conversation with Johnny. "Funny you should mention that. We were just talking about a name for the boat earlier today. I think we settled on Zombie Refuge."

"Yes, a fitting name for these days and times," Black Bart said as he typed. "When we are finished servicing

Zombie Refuge, we'll put it in . . ." he paused as he studied the screen. "Slip N53; that's Northside."

After verifying contact information and leaving a down payment for services to be rendered, Pacie took the business card and pamphlet that he handed both her and Irma.

"You ladies are welcome to attend the sailing lessons, too." Black Bart focused once again on Irma. "If you don't want to go through anything formal, I can give personal lessons. It is a good idea that all aboard the vessel be knowledgeable. Just call the number on the card and ask for me."

Pacie thought it was unusual for the harbormaster to offer his time and service to people he did not know. But it was obvious that he was attracted to Irma, and she to him.

They walked outside. Pacie studied the diagram and the slip that Bart had marked in the pamphlet as they made their way to the car. She stopped and looked back at the water and pointed to where she thought slip N53 was. "The slip is somewhere over there."

"He's a nice man." Irma kept walking, not paying attention to where Pacie was pointing.

Pacie smiled as they climbed inside the SUV. "If I didn't know better, I'd think you two kinda like each other."

Irma looked down. "He's okay."

"I think he's more than okay. Are you going to see him again? Maybe take a lesson?"

"I haven't been with a man in decades," Irma said as she fastened her seatbelt. "I don't have time to date. We have this hornet situation to take care of."

Pacie put the car in gear. "You can do both at the same time. It's not like you're getting married or something."

"Married? I think you're jumping the gun on that one."

"What I mean is that it would be nice if you had a friend. You don't want to hang out with your favorite cousin all your life, do you?"

"I'm satisfied with my life." Irma squirmed in her seat. "Besides, I'm set in my ways. Everything is where I want it—I can always find the channel changer, I don't have to wear a sweater because the thermostat is turned down to freezing, and I don't have to put up with beer cans and dirty dishes scattered around the apartment." Irma spoke as if she had experience in this area. "I don't want someone moving my stuff around, and I don't want to listen to football, or watch drag car racing."

Pacie nodded in agreement as she drove onto the road and headed to Sam's Family Restaurant. "I'm with Johnny and everything is fine."

"That's different."

"How?"

"I don't know, but it is. Besides, if I did see Bart again, I wouldn't know how to act."

"Okay, here's the big question. Do you want to see Bart again?"

"Maybe." Irma looked out the side window, away from Pacie.

"Based on the way you acted at the marina, I think you like him."

Irma glanced at Pacie. "What do you think of him?"

"Hmm. I think he seems like a nice guy. You should call him and take him up on a personal boating lesson. What could it hurt?"

Irma looked back at Mr. Dibble, who appeared to be engrossed in the conversation. Quietly, she turned and stared out the front window.

Pacie did not want to push the topic, but it would be nice if her cousin found someone special, even if Bart turned out to be nothing more than a friend that she could occasionally hang out with.

They pulled into Sam's and drove to the back of the lot near a large grassy yard by a cornfield. The brown brick building and red awnings revved up Pacie's appetite as she found a vacant spot near the dumpster. It was as busy as she expected for a late Thursday afternoon.

Irma let Mr. Dibble out for a short walk and to relieve himself. Pacie moseyed around the dumpster, looking for bigger than normal bees. All she found—among the stench of rotten food—was an emptied can of vegetables being used as an ashtray, apparently for staff on a smoke break.

With Mr. Dibble back inside the SUV, they entered the restaurant. A hungry family in line in front of them was being seated, exposing a collapsible A-frame sign listing Sam's daily specials. Handwritten in red on the whiteboard, today's specials were meatloaf and mashed potatoes, vegetarian lasagna, and strawberry pie.

Servers in black aprons and red polo shirts moved smoothly through the aisles. Pleasant conversation and the aroma of greasy french fries made Pacie hungrier.

A hostess that could be from the local college led them to a booth in the room with artificial ivy hanging in baskets from the ceiling near greenhouse-style windows. She laid a laminated menu in front of each of them. "Your server will be Evelyn. She'll be with you shortly."

Pacie delighted in the warm glow of the August sunlight streaming through the tinted glass. The view of the parking lot mattered little. She opened the menu and searched among the entrées for something that sounded good at the moment. When she looked at Irma across the table from her, it was difficult to tell if she was happy or sad. "Do you know what you're going to get?"

Irma shrugged. "Not yet."

A neighborly woman in her forties with short brown wavy hair approached the table. "Hi, I'm Evelyn, your server. Can I get you both something to drink?"

"I'll have an iced tea," Pacie said.

"Coffee," Irma blurted as she stared out the window.

"Thank you. I'll be back in a moment."

Pacie studied Irma. She could tell something was wrong. Aside from the fact that Irma was not talking—or complaining—and instead appeared caught in some type of daydream. "Wanna talk about it?"

"Nothing to talk about."

"Well, something's wrong. You're not being your normal self. It has to do with Bart, doesn't it? Do you already know him?"

Another uncharacteristic shrug. "No, I've never seen him before."

"Then what is it? You might as well come clean because I'm going to keep bugging you about it until you do."

Evelyn returned with their drinks. "Are you ready to order?"

"I am," Pacie said, looking back down at the stiff plastic menu. She thought of getting the daily special but instead decided on her usual. "I'll have the Sammy Burger basket."

Irma closed the menu and handed it to Evelyn. I'll have scrambled eggs with bacon and white toast."

Evelyn left with the order. Pacie put her elbows on the table and leaned toward Irma. "It's noisy in here. No one is going to hear what we're saying."

Irma fiddled with her coffee cup, twisting it this way and that. "Okay, I'll tell you."

Pacie said nothing as she listened.

"I don't think I've ever told you this before, but many years ago, when I was much younger, I was dating a guy that I thought would become my husband. He was loving, fun, and treated me like a princess. I even had a hope chest filled with table linens, a quilt that I sewed myself, and dishes handed down from Great-Grandma Foster." She sipped her coffee. "We were even engaged, that is, until this other woman came along. She was prettier, richer, and more cultured than me. He dropped me like a hot potato. I was devastated and sank into a deep depression—for a long time. Could hardly get out of bed and didn't want to."

"I'm sorry," Pacie said. "Are you afraid the same thing will happen with Bart?"

Another shrug. "I sold my house and moved here to Black Water. I didn't want to run into them again."

"I don't blame you." Pacie leaned back in the booth. "Do I know him?"

"No. Biff doesn't live in Black Water."

Pacie wanted to say something snarky about Irma having dated someone with the Back to the Future name of Biff, but that could wait for a better time. "I'm no expert in these matters, but let me ask you a question. When you drive—or ride—in a car, do you trust the drivers coming at you in the other lane? Trust that they're going to stay in their lane and not crash into you?"

"Yeah, of course I do."

"It's kind of the same thing with people. Just because that other guy was a jerk doesn't mean Bart is. I think you need to trust."

"Have you been listening to Tony Robbins?" Irma's tone had shifted to a more Irma-like grumble. "I see what you're getting at."

"Besides, if ol' Black Bart does anything to you, I'll send Johnny after him. I promise."

Irma laughed. "Okay, okay. It's just that these terrible memories were brought back, along with the old feelings."

"You look a little better. Aren't you glad we talked about it?"

Irma blew air out through puffed cheeks. "I'll be fine. But I still need to think about Bart."

"That's good enough for me."

"We should see Oscar tomorrow and see what he has to say about these big hornets," Irma said. She took her cellphone from her fanny pack. "If we get there early, we can catch him before he's busy with service calls." She slid through a couple of screens. "Oscar's Vermin Control opens at nine."

"Okay. I'll be at your place before that."

After chatting a bit longer on non-Bart topics, their food came—a red woven serving basket lined with black checkered deli paper and a heavy dinner plate filled with steaming hot eats.

Pacie noticed that Evelyn was distracted by something in the parking lot. Having just asked if they needed refills on their drinks, she stood still, her jaw lax.

"Is everything okay?" Pacie asked Evelyn.

The server slowly raised her arm and pointed out the window.

Pacie first looked at Irma, who had already dug into the belated breakfast, then out to the parking lot. Everything looked fine as a chatty family of four walked to their car; the youngest carried a foil birthday balloon as he blew a whistle. "What do you see?"

"Look." Evelyn pointed to a Japanese maple in front of the window. "What is that?"

Pacie looked to where Evelyn pointed, at first not noticing anything abnormal. Then she saw it, an oversized hornet perched among the chartreuse leaves of the dwarf tree next to the building. It appeared to be watching them. Now her jaw dropped. To Pacie's eye, it seemed to look directly at her. Was this the same giant hornet with a bent antenna that she saw at her house earlier? "No way. It's Auntie Bee."

Irma almost choked on the scrambled eggs when she caught sight of the mutant. "Auntie Bee? what are you talking about? There's possibly a killer bee just beyond the glass and you're giving it a cutesy name. Are you all right?"

"It just came to me," Pacie said, feeling silly. "What's really weird is that it looks like the same hornet that was on the hummingbird feeder."

Irma pushed her plate to the center of the table. "How can you tell?"

"It has a bent antenna . . . and it's looking directly at me."

"Are you saying it's intelligent?" Irma shoved her coffee cup away. "And that it's, for some reason, after you?"

"I'm just saying there's something more to that bee than its enormous size. I'm not sure why, it's just a feeling I get from it."

"That thing was at your house?" Evelyn asked as she crossed her arms over her chest as if she were tightening a shawl. "What exactly is it?"

"Some kind of large hornet." Pacie took her phone from her satchel, focused, and snapped a shot of the bug.

A crowd began gathering around them, trying to get a closer look at the insect. Gasps and comments of disbelief stood out among the chatter.

"I'm afraid to go outside," one woman said as the small child in her arms squirmed to escape her hold.

A man with a long beard pulled eyeglasses from his shirt pocket. "We're being invaded by alien wasps." He leaned across the table, almost knocking over Pacie's iced tea. "Or it's some kind of military project. I've read that the government has a secret project that looks at other ways to fight wars so that there is less risk to humans."

"It's a military plan gone wrong," Evelyn said, backing away.

Suddenly, the wasp lifted off the branch and joined two other large hornets as they flew toward the celebrating family of four as they were getting into their car. They screamed and swatted at the bees until finally safe inside the sedan.

"Call the police," someone yelled.

Evelyn took the cellphone from her back pocket and dialed 9-1-1.

"Mr. Dibble." Irma abruptly stood, her body striking the table, causing the drinks to spill. "I left the window cracked. Quick, give me your keys.

PART II

Where There's Smoke
There's Fire

5

Concoction

Pacie took the keys from her satchel and slid them across the table to Irma, then slapped more cash than necessary next to the salt and pepper shakers before chasing behind her.

When she reached the exit, she paused and looked through the glass for signs of Auntie Bee and her companions. Not seeing any, she shot through the door and ran to the SUV. Irma was already inside with Mr. Dibble. The family that the bees had attacked was speeding through the parking lot, roaring onto the road as if the hornets were going to chase them and their loud rust bucket all the way home.

Pacie jumped in the driver's seat and checked that the windows were all rolled up. "Are you two okay?"

Mr. Dibble was sitting awkwardly on Irma's lap as if he were a child needing protection. "We're fine. The hornets were more interested in the family and their noisy car than us."

"I think they're attracted to noise. Remember, you told me how they attacked that guy's lawnmower?"

Irma directed Mr. Dibble to the backseat. "That's right. We need one of those ultrasonic pest-repellent things."

Pacie looked at the clock on the dash. "It's five. We should head over to the pest control guy now because this bee thing is getting out of control."

"I'll call him while you drive there."

"It's on Tipton Road, isn't it?"

"Yeah, on the edge of town." Irma held the phone to her head. "Oscar, it's Irma."

"Irma. Haven't heard from you in a while. How's the investigation business going?"

"Well, that's why I'm calling. You may already know this, but there are abnormally large hornets around town and they're attacking people."

"I do know about it. I've gotten a few calls and have been out to a couple of places in town but haven't seen them myself, just eyewitness accounts of these hornets that are the size of a small bird."

"Pacie and I are heading your way now. Are you gonna be there?"

"I'll be in the back of the shop."

"See you soon."

The drive to Oscar's was uneventful. Other than fewer people than normal out in their yards, the traffic was the same as any summer day in the resort town.

"There it is, Oscar's Vermin Control," Irma said, pointing to a weathered sign that needed to be repainted. Ironically, faded bees made up the peeling border.

Pacie pulled onto the gravel driveway, flanked by tall, neglected grass. The shop was a converted garage next to a house that needed repainting as badly as the sign near the road. Pacie had the impression that Oscar's business was struggling to make ends meet.

The three of them hopped out of the car. Irma put the leash on Mr. Dibble and walked to the shop door as a long-haired collie came around the corner of the house and barked at them, keeping its distance while it wagged its tail as if unsure if it was a guard dog or the friendly, family pooch. Mr. Dibble walked calmly next to his master, ignoring the conflicted dog.

The shop sign on the door window displayed SORRY WE'RE CLOSED. Irma rapped on the doorframe twice and stepped inside. The shop smelled of chemicals and mothballs. Shelves on the walls held items from what looked like homemade birdhouses to jugs of pesticides.

"Are you here, Oscar?" Irma called out.

"I'm back here," he shouted.

They walked to the open door behind the counter, which led into his workshop. Oscar—a skinny, frail-looking man dressed in shabby clothes—was mixing chemicals like a mad scientist, combining a little of this with a little of that into a two-liter glass container over the bluish flame of a Bunsen burner.

Pacie's first thought questioned how cancerous those chemicals were that Oscar was fumbling around with. The plastic containers looked years old, as though he had pulled them off a dusty shelf in a back corner of the shop before safety regulations were in effect.

"What are you doing?" Irma asked as they stepped deeper into the chemistry lab.

"Based on the descriptions I've received by panicked callers; I'm creating a mixture that should work better on the flyin' freaks than the standard formulas out there."

"Is it toxic?" Pacie asked, watching an ungloved Oscar stir the concoction.

"Only to the hornets." Oscar laughed. "What I'm makin' isn't cancer-causing creosote or the tumor makin' DDT. It's safe—as far as I know—and needed in this situation."

"Have you ever heard of bees like this before?" Pacie knew he was an experienced exterminator, but she had never spoken with him.

"They sound like an unknown variety of Vespa mandarinia. . . Asian murder hornets. But to know for sure I need a specimen. If you can catch me one, preferably alive, I'll be able to tell."

"That might be hard, but we'll give it our best shot," Pacie said, wondering why he was asking ordinary citizens to catch a potentially life-threatening hornet. But then, she and Irma were not ordinary citizens, they were citizen investigators who—to the chagrin of the local police department—routinely broke the rules and got themselves into precarious situations. "Any advice on how we can do that without getting stung?"

"A wasp trap should work. I have them here, but if they're as big as everyone says, the trap might need some modifyin'. As far as bait, the kits come with it. But if you want to make your own, you can use a sweet liquid like fruit juice, water with jam . . . basically sugar water. In the spring, hunks of meat like hamburger works well."

Pacie shook her head. "Why am I not surprised that these overgrown bugs like fresh meat?"

Oscar continued, "I'm going to use pheromone bait that attracts queen hornets. And if anyone finds what they think is a nest, I have a thermal-imaging device to spot heat signatures from a distance."

"Okay," Pacie said, "we'll take a couple of your wasp traps."

"These are nasty critters," Oscar said, measuring a gray liquid into his brew. "Normally they're the size of a whole thumb; with a stinger that is a quarter inch long. That's a giant in its own right. But based on what I've been hearing, the ones here in Black Water are different; they're much bigger and aggressive."

"They're also smarter," Pacie said.

Oscar looked up from his work. "Smarter?"

"Well, I don't know this for sure, but I think I've seen the queen like twice and I get the feeling it's stalking me."

"That is quite interesting," Oscar said. "And extremely disturbing. They sound like they've been genetically modified."

"Oh wait, I almost forgot," Pacie said, retrieving her phone. "I took a picture of the one I saw at Sam's Family Restaurant."

Oscar took the phone Pacie handed him. He twitched as he studied the picture. "This is very distressing. Send this to the Michigan Department of Agriculture and let me know what they say if they happen to contact you."

"Will do."

Mr. Dibble sniffed along the floor near a stainless-steel sprayer and wand. Irma pulled him back, then said, "We know that noise attracts them and makes them angry. They've attacked a lawnmower and a family with a child blowing a whistle."

"I'm not surprised." Oscar turned off the gas burner and gave his brew a final stir. "I'll let this cool down. In the meantime, let's get you two a couple of wasp catchers."

After using a pocketknife to modify the hole—and cut his thumb—he handed the traps to them.

"We'll get these hung out today," Irma said. "Let us know if you discover something that we need to report. Our contact information is on the website."

"Don't you worry, I will." Oscar put the knife back in his pocket. "Call me as soon as you attract anything interesting. I'll come out to the house so that you don't have to handle whatever you catch."

"Thank you, Oscar," Irma said as they left the exterminator's lab.

The collie that barked at them earlier now lay in the cool grass panting as it watched them walk back to the car.

Pacie's phone rang as they climbed into the SUV.

"Hi, Char, how's it going?" Pacie said to her granddaughter as she fastened her seatbelt.

An anxious Char said, "Grandma, are there really killer bees in Black Water? I heard they chased people in Sam's parking lot."

Pacie's first thought was how fast bad news travels. Her second thought was that everyone needed to be on the lookout for the hornets. "I was going to call you and your mom. Are you at home right now?"

"No. Renee and I are at the beach watching them set up for InkyFest. Why?"

A twinge of dread shot through Pacie. "Well, you're right, there have been sightings of big hornets. If you see them, don't make any noise to attract them. You're not allergic to bees, are you?"

"No."

"You and Renee should head home until we figure out how to get rid of them."

Charlotte sighed. "Ok."

"Is your mom home?"

"She should be."

"Ok, Irma and I are heading over to your house. See you soon."

Irma had already lit a cigarette. "This might be a problem."

"What?"

"InkyFest; it's on Saturday. Hornets and festivals don't mix."

"Crap. You're right. Loud music, lots of people, and those monsters flying around are a dangerous combination."

"It should be canceled."

"I think it's too late. Besides, the bee events have been so isolated that no one would listen anyway."

"I'll call the TV station and the paper. They can at least put out a warning." Irma took her cell phone from her fanny pack.

"I think we could have a real disaster on our hands," Pacie said as she drove down the driveway.

6

Queen

"There's only one car in the driveway," Irma said. "Char must not be back yet."

"She's probably taking her friend home," Pacie said as she pulled next to her son-in-law's beat-up blue pickup truck he uses to drive to work.

By the time they reached the side entrance, her daughter, Amanda Booth, had the door open for them.

"Come on in," Amanda said. "You're just in time for supper."

Mr. Dibble stayed outside in the familiar yard while Pacie and Irma entered the spicy aroma of the kitchen.

Theodore took the last bite of the enchilada on his plate. "Are you hungry? There're leftovers."

Considering her Sammy Burger Basket was left uneaten at Sam's, Pacie was starving, but she did not want to intrude. "Thanks, but we're not staying. We just wanted to talk about the latest news to befall our curious town of Black Water."

"Curious? You mean damned," Theodore said as he took his plate to the sink. He wet a paper towel and wiped red sauce from his t-shirt and the top of his beer belly. "What is it this time? A serial killer? Werewolves? Alternate dimensions?"

"Theo, this is serious," Amanda said as she wiped the dining table. "I haven't paid much attention to the news lately, but I hope it's not too serious."

Pacie sat on a dining chair while Irma looked out the side door window. "It's not serious yet, but it could become a big problem."

Theodore sat across from Pacie. "What is it? What's going on?"

"There are some rather large bees in town. They seem to be aggressive, too."

Amanda rinsed the dishrag in the sink and sat down. "How worried should we be? Has anyone been hurt?"

"No one has been hurt, as far as I know, but I wouldn't want to be stung by one of them."

"Just how big are they?" Theo asked.

Pacie explained everything she knew about the hornets, then added, "I'd recommend not doing noisy things like mowing the lawn or even going to the Inky Festival this weekend where there's going to be loud music."

"Considering these hornets have only scared people and not actually hurt anyone, I don't think letting our lawn grow into a jungle is desirable." Theodore laughed. "Besides, if they're as big as you say they are, they should be easy to spot. Has Harborfest been canceled?"

"No, it hasn't," Pacie said.

A car door closed.

"That must be Char," Amanda said.

Char and Mr. Dibble walked into the kitchen. She hugged Irma and Pacie. "Is everything okay? I mean are the bees out of control?"

"Right now, everything is . . . I wouldn't say under control. . . being monitored," Pacie said.

"I hope the festival isn't canceled because I want to go there with my friends and watch Bad Credit. They're a band out of Lolly." Char looked at her mom. "I can still go, can't I?"

"We'll play it by ear," Amanda said.

"I would recommend not going," Pacie said, knowing she was sounding like an old grump.

Irma leaned against the kitchen counter, looking at her phone. "There's a new report that a local beekeeper lost a colony of his honeybees. Looks like something attacked them. They were decapitated."

"That's not a good sign," Pacie said. "I think murder hornets do things like that."

Amanda gasped. "Murder hornets? You didn't say anything about that."

Pacie knew she had chosen her words poorly. "We don't know what they are. Traps are set so that we can catch one, and then Oscar, the exterminator guy, can determine what it is."

Amanda turned to Char, who was walking into the living room. "Char, maybe you should stay home for a while, at least until we figure this out."

Char stopped in her tracks. "Mom. Really? Like Grandma said, we don't know what they are."

"I'll let you know the moment I find out anything." Pacie stood and rubbed the back of her neck. "It's been a long day and I'm exhausted. Can't wait to crawl into bed."

"Before you go, take some chocolate chip cookies. Char made them this morning." Amanda placed three chunky cookies into Ziploc bags.

"These look delicious," Pacie said, taking one of the much-appreciated baggies.

Char came into the kitchen. "Bye, Grandma. Don't get stung. Bye, Irma. You two—I mean three—be safe."

"Don't worry, we'll be careful as usual," Pacie said, knowing that was not entirely the truth. She gave Char another hug.

"Come on, Mr. Dibble, time to go," Irma said as she opened the door. "Bye everyone."

When they were back in the SUV, Pacie said, "We should visit the beekeeper tomorrow morning. Where's he at?"

"He owns Handy's Orchard, just outside town," Irma said, looking at her phone. "I'll contact Mr. Handy and let him know we'll be out there."

"We should talk to a government agency tomorrow, too," Pacie said. "I'll send the picture I have to the Department of Agriculture when I get home . . . after I find their email address."

"I don't think they have an office in Black Water," Irma said, flipping through screens. "Mention in the email that we'll do a Zoom or Skype call with them, because it looks like their office is in Lansing."

After what seemed like a long-drawn-out drive to Irma's apartment, they finally reached the parking lot. When Irma and Mr. Dibble got out, she looked up to Johnny's third-floor apartment. A light was on, but she was too tired to visit. She would instead head straight home.

Shadows were growing long when Pacie arrived at the mansion. She dragged herself inside and into her study. After a quick search, she found the Michigan Department of Agriculture and Rural Development's email address and sent them a copy of the picture she took of Auntie Bee, along with a note listing the facts as she knew them.

After hanging the bee trap outside the little parlor window near the hummingbird feeder, and eating a home-baked cookie, Pacie went upstairs to her bedroom and got ready for bed. She plopped onto the mattress, covered herself with a sheet, and fell almost immediately to sleep.

* * *

The roar of a chainsaw woke Pacie. After coming to, she realized that what she was hearing was not teeth on a chain, powered by a two-stroke engine, but the buzz of a bee.

The room was darker than usual, and she had difficulty locating the sound. All she knew was that it was moving around the bed as if taunting her. Was it one of those giant hornets? And how did it get in her bedroom?

She wanted to cover her head and cower under the sheet like a child, fearing the monster in the closet. But she knew the thin material would offer no protection against what had to be a very long stinger.

Her body told her not to move, to lie still and wait until it went away, or it landed on her, at which time she would deal with it. But her mind told her she had to move, had to make the first move before being stung, and probably dying.

Her cellphone was on the bedside stand. She would grab it and run to the bathroom, where she would close the door and be safe.

With the plan set in her mind, she took a deep breath, and without further thought, reached quickly for the phone, knocking it to the floor. She fumbled for the light switch and, in her haste, knocked the adjustable arm lamp to the floor.

The buzzing had stopped. Where was the hornet? Was it on the floor where she could step on it as she ran for the door, or was it resting on a doorknob, waiting for her grasp?

Her eyes had adjusted to the darkness. A diffuse light illuminated only the outlines of objects directly in the window's moon glow. She needed more light. As far as Pacie saw it, she had three options: lay quiet as a mouse until morning, run out of the room to safety, or kill the insect.

Part of her wanted to go back to sleep and forget about it. It had to be a nightmare; it just had to be. Then she remembered the hardcover novel on the nightstand shelf. It could be used to whack the creature. Pacie reached for the heavy book, fearing she would grab the hornet, but instead she found an empty shelf.

What the heck? Where is the book? At the rate things are going, my EpiPen will be missing, too. But my purse is downstairs in the study, anyway.

Pacie would have to walk to one of the room's overhead light switches located by all three doors: the door to the secondary staircase, the bathroom, and the door leading through to the chintz room.

The buzzing started up again. It was loud and moving by the door to the staircase. If she was able to make it to the bathroom, she would be trapped. Escaping through the chintz room was her best bet.

Past the glow of the moon, the room was black as death. But Pacie knew the room as well as a blind man. With what had to be Auntie Bee still guarding the staircase, Pacie sprinted to the closed door leading into a small room that passed into the other bedroom. She fumbled with the knob, trying to open the door. With frantic jiggling, she was finally able to unlatch it and dash inside the pass-through, slamming the door behind her.

How did that bee even get inside the house? Pacie said aloud as she went through the door leading into the chintz room.

With her back against the door, the bedroom was no less dark. She rushed forward toward the door on the other side of the room but stopped and winced in pain when she stubbed her toe on the bed's leg. She continued moving through the door and into the second-floor hallway.

Auntie Bee had to be trapped in her bedroom. She would go down to the study, grab her purse and make sure the auto-injector was inside.

As Pacie limped down the staircase to the first floor, she heard someone rummaging through items in her study. It wasn't a bee; it had to be a person. She stopped on the landing, trying to figure out her next course of action.

It was probably Irma because she had a key to the mansion, as did Johnny, Amanda, Theodore, and Char. But it was also possible that a thief was inside the house looking for something valuable.

Her heart was still racing as she quietly descended the main staircase and entered the dining room. She felt her way past the dining table to the door on the other side that led to a small room and into the study. As she entered the butler's pantry, she saw a man through the open door to the study, mumbling as though upset with himself for not finding something. It wasn't Johnny or Theodore.

"Oscar?"

The exterminator, dressed in his pajamas and a backpack sprayer, turned to her. "Where is it?"

He looked tired, his face drawn, and to Pacie's horror there was a hornet on his shoulder, a large hornet. Pacie gasped as she pointed toward it. "There— there's a bee on you. Don't move."

"Oh, don't worry about her," Oscar said. "She just wants to meet you."

"I don't want to meet it," Pacie said, taking a step back. "What are you doing in my house? How did you get in here?"

Oscar reached up and patted the insect. "I'm looking for the epinephrine. Where is it?"

"What? My EpiPen? Why?" Pacie looked at the pink bunny slippers on Oscar's feet. Something was wrong. This is all wrong.

"She told me. The queen." Oscar stepped toward Pacie. "She doesn't want you to have the medicine. It's not in her best interest."

Pacie stepped back, ready to slam the door closed. "Oscar, you're making no sense. You're sleepwalking."

Oscar smiled. "I'm not walking in my sleep. I just need you to listen to me."

"You want me dead?" Pacie could not believe she was having this conversation. "Because if I were to get stung, I would go into anaphylactic shock if I don't have my pen."

"That's the point," Oscar said. "If you're alive, you will stop the queen and her family from setting up shop in Black Water. They need to live, and I need to work with them. To study them."

Pacie shook when Oscar whistled and a swarm of hornets at once surrounded him as if he were lord of bees. The room buzzed like an out of tune orchestra. Then, with a click of his fingers, the throng of wasps shot toward her before she could retreat back into the dining room.

7

Headless

Pacie awoke with a start; her perspiration-soaked nightgown clung to her chest. She gasped for air until she realized that what she was imagining must have been a dream. Safe in her bed, there were no hornets attacking her.

Startled by the ring of her cellphone—on the nightstand where she had left it—she shook her head, relieved the experience was a nightmare and not a home intrusion. She picked up the phone, her hand trembled.

"Hi, Irma." Pacie knew she sounded stressed.

"Are you okay?"

Pacie sighed. "I'm fine. I had a weird dream last night. It felt so real."

"I bet it was about hornets."

"Yeah, hornets and Oscar."

"You dreamed of Oscar?"

"He was in my house looking for my EpiPen and he had Auntie Bee on his shoulder."

"That's bizarre."

"He was in his pajamas and bunny slippers, and he wanted—I mean, the queen wanted me dead. So he sicked a swarm of hornets on me."

Irma laughed. "Oscar wouldn't harm a fly, so to speak."

"I know; it is rather ridiculous. So what's up?"

"Mr. Handy emailed me back and wants us to go out to the orchard and see if we can figure out why his honeybees were decapitated."

"It's really weird that something chopped off their poor little heads."

"He's expecting to see us this morning," Irma said. "I did some research and found that murder hornets' prey on honeybees. They bite off their heads, leaving the adults in piles while carrying young bees back to their nest to feed their young. A few dozen hornets can kill a whole hive in just a few hours."

"Feed their young?" Pacie said, pulling her sweat-drenched nightgown away from her skin. "That means they're growing in number. This is bad news. We have to find their nest."

"I shot Oscar an email about it," Irma said. "Did you get your wasp trap hung?"

"I did. I put it by the hummingbird feeder since that's where we saw one of them. How about you?"

"Johnny hung it up for me yesterday. We'll check it when you get here."

Pacie stood up on weak knees. "I'll be over to pick you up as soon as I get around."

After a quick shower and a fresh brew of Columbian coffee for her to-go cup, Pacie checked the wasp trap outside the parlor window. She had not caught the sample that Oscar needed for his special blend of chemicals.

Pacie walked outside into the fresh Friday morning air. She half wished it was raining because it might ground the hornets from flight, but she did not know this to be a fact.

As she drove to Irma's, the news on the radio reported several sightings of larger than normal bees and frightened citizens, but as of yet no reports of stings. But Pacie knew it was coming; it was just a matter of time. And when that time comes, it could lead to many deaths.

The reports were merely sightings, with mention of the aggressive nature of the insects. The newscaster played a recording of Irma advising the citizens to avoid the monsters and to not do anything to aggravate them, like making loud noises or doing anything that might be deemed threatening by the hornets.

"Good job, Irma," Pacie said as she pulled into the apartment's parking lot. She looked at her watch; it was a little after nine. Johnny would be in the shop.

Pacie parked and walked into the antique store's backdoor. Johnny was dusting a shelf filled with trinkets.

"Oh, wow, it's nice seeing a man taking care of domestic chores," Pacie said as she walked up to him.

"Don't get your hopes up, sweetheart." Johnny sat the feather duster on the glass shelf and put his hands around her waist. "This is simply business."

Pacie kissed him. "I think you're trainable."

"Like a monkey?"

"Maybe." She smiled.

Johnny kept his arms wrapped around her waist. "I don't think monkeys can be house-trained. I heard they urinate and defecate wherever they want—in the corner, on your bed, in your shoes."

"Okay, you're not a tailed primate. I'll have to think on it."

"So," Johnny said, squinting at her. "Don't tell me you and Irma are going bee hunting."

"Technically, no."

"No? Then why was I hanging a wasp trap for your cousin yesterday?"

"Hornets aren't technically bees; they're a stinging wasp. And yes, Irma and I are investigating them. These insects are big and multiplying. I think they're becoming dangerous."

"That sounds nice. Why can't you hunt butterflies or mushrooms?"

"Good question."

"I might not let you leave," Johnny said, pulling her closer. "You're allergic to bee venom, and what would I do if something were to happen to you? Who would help me with domestic woman's work?"

Pacie fake punched him in the side. "Maybe I'll stop helping so that you're forced to learn this *so-called* woman's work of which you speak."

"I'm just picking on you. But seriously, you shouldn't be anywhere around bees or hornets or anything like that. Do you have your EpiPen with you?"

Pacie tapped her satchel. "It's in here, along with my phone."

The front door shopkeeper's bell jingled.

Johnathon kissed her again. "Promise me you'll be careful."

"I always am."

"Why don't I believe that?"

Johnathon left to tend to the customers while Pacie walked to the back of the shop and took the creaky staircase to the second floor and Irma's apartment. She rapped the door a couple of times and walked inside. Irma was sitting at her desk with Mr. Dibble lying on a rug next to her ergonomic chair.

"Black Water has a problem," Irma said, leaning back and swiveling toward Pacie.

"I know," Pacie said, walking up to her. "It won't be long and people will start dying."

"When we're done seeing Mr. Handy, we should stop at the mayor's office and see if he'll cancel or at least postpone InkyFest until this bee thing is under control."

"If we can get it under control." Pacie pushed a hand crocheted blanket aside and sat on the couch. "But there's one problem."

"What, besides the obvious?"

"Mayor Castleman won't cancel it; he's too . . ."

"Dimwitted?"

Pacie grinned. "He'd say the show must go on even as a swarm of hornets were attacking the crowd."

"Ain't that the truth? The mayor has no commonsense, but he does bring a lot of tourists and business to town." Irma typed on the keyboard. "I'm sending an email to the mayor's office to let them know we'll be out to see him today."

Pacie looked at her phone. "I emailed the Department of Agriculture yesterday and haven't heard back yet. You'd think this was something they would want to jump on."

Irma stood. "Are you ready to go to the orchard?"

"Let's do it."

They walked outside and checked the wasp trap that Johnny had hung on a ginkgo tree between the building and the parking lot.

Pacie looked at the trap hanging nicely between the fan-shaped leaves. "You needed Johnny's help to hang this?"

"I wasn't sure." Irma shrugged.

Pacie knew Irma asked Johnny for help often: getting something from the top of her closet, moving furniture, or hanging a picture. Fortunately, Johnny did not care. He laughed about it when he told her of the services he rendered. He knew Irma only had family she could call for help, but Johnny was the closest and most convenient person. "I don't see a hornet or anything else in it."

"It hasn't been up that long. We can check it again later."

The three climbed into Pacie's SUV and drove to Handy's Orchard just outside town. It was hard to believe Black Water was on the verge of a disaster as they passed an Amish horse-drawn buggy, fields of corn, and white-tailed deer grazing along a distant tree line.

Soon they approached acres of fruit trees loaded with tart Garya Red, Ginger Gold, and the latest to harvest, spicy-sweet Braeburn apples. A tractor mowed between straight lines of pruned trees.

"Maybe we can get a peck or half peck of apples before we leave," Pacie said as she pulled onto the gravel driveway. "An apple pie sounds good."

"I don't think the apples are ripe yet. It'll be a few more weeks for the earliest ones."

The country store was like a farmers' market, with bushels of fruit and vegetables on display, along with wind chimes, painted garden images, and the distant crow of a rooster from the nearby red barn.

Irma put Mr. Dibble on his leash, and they walked to the porch with white rails resting on wooden posts. Even though the apples had not been harvested, there were near overflowing baskets on tables filled with peaches, nectarines, and raspberries, ready for purchase. A rocking chair and hanging baskets of ivy gave a homey and welcoming appearance.

Pacie picked up one of the clear plastic totes filled with a blush of peaches as they walked into the store. Mr. Handy was behind the counter.

"Ladies, I wish I were seeing you under better circumstances, but I've lost half my honeybee hives. They're invaluable to the orchard, as you know. This will have a detrimental impact on my produce. I've never seen anything like it in my life."

"I'm sorry to hear that," Pacie said. "After I pay for this, can you take us to one of the hives?"

Mr. Handy rung up the peaches. "Dale, can you watch the counter for me? I'm going to be out in the field."

"Sure thing, Mr. Handy." The young man wore a white canvas apron with Handy's Orchard embroidered across the chest. He stopped stocking jars of homemade jam onto a shelf and reached down and patted Mr. Dibble on the head. "Hey, Mr. Dibble. How are you?"

Mr. Handy took his apron off and hung it on a back wall peg next to the office door. "Do you ladies have your walking shoes on?"

Irma pointed toward bee suits hanging on a rack. "Pacie, you should probably get some protective gear."

"It won't be necessary," Mr. Handy said. "There are no live bees where I'm taking you."

Pacie put the peaches in the car and followed Mr. Handy across the driveway. Gravel crunched under their feet. The rooster crowed again as they walked toward the orchard.

"I thought roosters crowed in the morning," Pacie said.

Mr. Handy's pace was quick for an old man. "The morning announcement at sunrise is the most common. Sometimes they crow if they sense danger or a threat to their territory. But every now and then they crow just because they feel like it."

Pacie laughed. But she could not help but wonder if hornets would attack the flock and if the rooster was putting out an alarm crow.

"Let's stop at the chicken coop," Mr. Handy said. "I want to make sure everything is all right."

They walked to the raised hen house next to the barn. The two-story coop looked like a miniature barn housed inside the safety of the chicken wire fence. A hen was walking up a plank to the nesting boxes.

"What the hell?" Mr. Handy said as he rushed into the gated yard housing the hens. Along the side of one of the coop's legs was a hole a foot deep, surrounded by pieces of shredded combs.

"What happened?" Pacie asked as she cautiously leaned over the scorched earth.

"The hens tore up a ground hornets' nest," Mr. Handy said as he pushed the debris aside with his boot. "They do the same thing when they find baby mice, rats, and moles. They can be pretty badass."

"Must be their inner dinosaur coming out." Pacie chuckled.

Irma took a Ziploc bag from her fanny pack and put a small piece of the hornets' nest inside. "Let's give this to Oscar; it might help him solve the big bee problem."

"I don't see any giant hornets," Pacie said. She looked at Mr. Handy. "Have you seen any abnormally big wasps lately?"

He took a blue tartan handkerchief from his back pocket and blew his nose. "Nope. But I have heard they've been sighted in the area."

"Let's get to that beehive you want to show us," Pacie said.

They walked through ankle-high grass and white Dutch clover to the first hive, a standing white rectangular structure made of wood.

Mr. Handy took the top off and pulled out a frame filled with combs of honey. He disassembled it, as dead bees fell to the ground. "What do you ladies make of this? I have near fifty hives across the orchard and half of them have been destroyed like this one."

Irma looked closely at the beheaded little bodies. "You're right; they've been decapitated."

"Of course. Now, can you tell me something that I don't already know?"

Irma looked at him. "We believe these hornets, the ones that have invaded Black Water, are Asian giant hornets. A trait of theirs is to decapitate honeybees and take their protein-rich bodies back to their nest to feed their young."

"I know a bit about bees, and these so-called murder hornets are not native to this area. And if they are as big as people are saying, they can't be the hornets that are native to Asia."

"We think they're mutants," Pacie said. "We have no idea how they got here nor exactly why they're as big as small birds. But we are trying to trap one of them so that we can take it to Oscar at Oscar's Vermin Control so that he can make a pesticide that will kill them."

Mr. Handy retrieved his hankie again. "If these hornets are as big as everyone says, how are they getting in through the small holes of the entrance reducer? It's purposely made that way so that the honeybees have a better chance of protecting the hive."

Irma thought a moment. "I assume they have a caste system of workers and drones. The workers might be able to squeeze through the opening."

Mr. Handy blew into the square cloth. "It's a damned plight to live on a farm and be plagued with allergies." He shoved the kerchief back into his pocket. "I don't know. I have a hard time believing these bizarre insects can get inside. But if they're mutants like you say, who knows what they can do?"

They stood there a moment, staring at the carnage.

"The other weird thing," Mr. Handy said, "is that some hives were knocked over and the supers and frames were scattered about, making it easy to get to the bees. I'll need to strap my surviving hives. Not to protect them from storms and skunks, but from these muscular hornets."

Pacie nodded. "It seems these invasive hornets are intelligent, strong, aggressive, and able to squeeze through small spaces. What else can they do?"

Mr. Handy wiped his watery eyes. "Okay. So what do I do in the meantime; until we can get rid of these things?"

Pacie looked at her phone for messages. "I sent an email to the Department of Agriculture and haven't heard back yet. I'm gonna have to give them a call. So in the meantime, I would suggest letting your staff know about these hornets and their aggressive nature and to not go near them. I would also recommend that you contact the Michigan Beekeepers Association and tell them everything you know."

"I can do that. I'll also contact the Lolly Area Beekeepers Association and see what they have to say."

Irma flipped through her cellphone, then stopped. "According to this, these Asian hornets send out a scout who hunts for food—honeybees are their favorite. Once they find a hive, they create pheromones that direct their nest mates to the hive. They have huge mandibles that they use to decapitate the honeybees. They can wipe out an entire colony."

Mr. Handy began putting the hive back together. "But like you said, these aren't normal bees. If these are mutants, like you say, not only are my pollinators in trouble, but the whole area could be doomed. Even the whole state. Hell, the entire country could be in bad shape if these mutants take over. Not only will they affect food production, but people's lives."

"Exactly," Pacie said. "We'll keep you informed of any new info we find."

"I appreciate that," Mr. Handy said. "But I've got a bad feeling about all this. Things could take a turn for the worse in a matter of hours."

Pacie nodded. "That's what I'm worried about. Our next stop is the mayor's office because InkyFest is tomorrow and there's going to be lots of people and loud music."

"Good luck with that," Mr. Handy said as he turned to walk back to the house. "Mayor Castleman isn't the easiest person to talk to. But the townsfolk love him, and so do the media."

"Yeah, he is quite the character," Pacie said, not looking forward to the visit.

8

Mayor

Pacie parked in front of the City of Black Water Offices. Posters advertising the Harborside Jamboree were taped on the front window of the downtown office building.

"I'm not looking forward to this," Irma said. "I don't think I've ever been able to change his mind about anything."

"Let's just go and get this over with," Pacie said as she opened the car door.

Mr. Dibble wanted to get out with Irma. "You stay here. I'll be right back."

The Staffordshire terrier had heard this phrase many times. He settled on the ragged blanket that Pacie kept on the backseat for him.

Pacie and Irma walked inside and knocked on the frame of the open door to the left.

The clerk, a woman in her thirties, wearing a dark blue tee shirt with InkyFest printed on the front, sat behind the desk. She looked up from typing and smiled. "Pacie, Irma, come on in. The mayor is in his office, but he'll be skedaddling soon to eat lunch. I told him you'd be stopping in this afternoon."

"Thanks, Helen," Pacie said. She looked at the clock on the wall. "I'd like to stay and chat, but I see it's close to lunch hour and I want to catch the mayor before he leaves."

They walked down the hall, past offices for public works, parks & rec, planning commission, and more. Mayor Castleman's office had a large sign above the door identifying him as the top executive in town.

The mayor walked out of his office door as they approached. He smiled. "You almost missed me. I was on my way to the café next door, but I have a few minutes for the both of you. Come into my office and we'll talk."

They walked inside and sat in two chic armless chairs positioned directly in front of his stately mahogany desk. His office was decorated with a nautical theme: a lighthouse candleholder, a ship's anchor wall plaque, and various other marine decor filled the room. The historical pictures of Black Water that hung from the paneled walls gave the impression that the historical society decorated the office.

"So, what's on your mind?" The mayor asked as he leaned back in his desk chair.

Pacie looked at Irma and back at the mayor. "I'm sure you've heard of the giant hornets that have invaded our town of Black Water."

"I have indeed."

"Well, it's our opinion that the festival tomorrow should be canceled. These hornets are—"

"Can't do it," the mayor snapped. "I know you're going to tell me that people could get stung by them, but as of yet, no one has. Besides, the weather is going to be warm and sunny, perfect for InkyFest. People are looking forward to it, and so am I."

"But mayor," Pacie protested. "These are huge bees and if anyone does get stung, they could die. Plus, they're attracted to loud sounds like bands playing."

"And you know this for a fact?"

"Well, not exactly, but that's what's been reported on the news, and we saw them chase a noisy car. Both of us have seen them . . . twice."

Pacie wanted to mention that Oscar was worried enough about them that he was developing a pesticide to kill them, but she was afraid that the mayor would report him to the EPA or whoever governs such matters.

"I haven't seen any. No one's been hurt by them. And the festival is on track to draw a record crowd. It would be premature to cancel anything."

Irma spoke up. "We just came from Handy's Orchard, and many of his beehives have been destroyed."

"By these giant bees?"

"We assume so," Irma said.

"I can't cancel one of the largest moneymakers in our town based on assumptions. I think you're being a little too cautious."

Pacie knew they weren't making their case. "Mayor Castleman, can you at least postpone it until we get a handle on these hornets?"

He paused a moment, as if considering the request. "I just can't do it. Everything is set for tomorrow. Besides, I did get an email from the Department of Agriculture and the Department of Health asking me about the hornets. I told them the little bit I knew. They gave no recommendations to cancel or postpone anything."

Pacie audibly sighed. "They were just info seeking?"

"It was very generic."

"Did they mention if these hornets have been seen anywhere else?"

"No, they didn't. So based on that, I don't see a reason to change anything. I'm sure they would've told me if the hornets were something to worry about."

"But these are huge hornets." Pacie felt like raising her voice, but she kept her cool. "I think they're dangerous. I think they're intelligent, strong, and lethal."

Irma handed the mayor her phone with the picture that Pacie had taken the day before. "We took that picture at Sam's Restaurant. It's one of the hornets."

The mayor studied the picture and then handed the phone back to Irma. "That is certainly a big bee, but there just isn't enough evidence to prove that they're dangerous. Until you provide that to me, I'm not changing anything."

"Can you put up signs or make an announcement to at least watch for them and report them if any are seen?" Pacie said.

"I'll think about it, but it's already been reported on the news. People can make their own judgement as to what to do." The mayor leaned forward and put his elbows on the desk. "You two have a good reputation in town and are *usually* correct in your assessments, but sometimes you're wrong. Like the time you said that a rash of tornadoes was coming through town, like the Apocalypse in the Bible— the end of the world kind of thing." The mayor rolled his eyes. "The worst we got was some mild straight-line wind. Aside from lawn furniture being blown around, there wasn't any damage."

Pacie knew he was right. They had made some bad judgments in the past, but they were errors on the side of caution.

"Most of the time you two are right on," the mayor said as he stood. "But you're not God or a prophet."

"I know I'm not. I can't believe you just said that." Pacie was annoyed and wanted to pound a fist on the desktop. "These bees could kill someone; maybe even a child."

"You're being a little dramatic, don't you think?" The mayor put a hand on his stomach when an audible growl was heard. "I'm going to the deli. Do you want to join me?"

Joining the mayor was the last thing Pacie wanted to do. "Thanks, but we have work to do."

Mayor Castleman motioned them toward the door. "Call me if you happen to find *legit* evidence that these bees are dangerous."

Pacie felt her blood rise to a simmer. Neither she nor Irma said anything as they walked down the hall and out the front door. They quickly climbed into the SUV.

"He hasn't changed," Irma said. She reached into her fanny pack and pulled out the bag with a piece of the ground hornets' nest inside. "Let's head over to Oscar's so that I can give him this."

Pacie was thinking of options; what they could do to keep the citizens safe. Even as a part of her thought that maybe the mayor was right. Maybe the hornets were gentle giants, and everything would be fine.

9

Of All People

Pacie drove to the nearest convenience store. "I need something to drink before we head to Oscar's."

"There's that guy," Irma said, pointing toward the diesel fuel pumps on the other side of the parking lot.

"Who?"

"That truck driver."

"Great. I hope I don't see him in the store."

Pacie and Irma walked inside and down an aisle to the back coolers. Irma took two bottles of cold water from a shelf while Pacie kept glancing around the store for any sign of the trucker; she did not want to run into him.

Pacie grabbed an ice tea as her cellphone beeped. "It's the Department of Agriculture."

"What did they say?"

"I don't know," Pacie said, fumbling with the icy bottle and her phone. She walked down the snack aisle toward the checkout counter with her focus on the email.

"Pacie, watch—"

With a thud and a groan, Pacie ran into what felt like a padded brick wall, but instead was a solid person. The phone, her tea, and dribbles of what appeared to be coffee fell to the tile floor. She looked up to see who she had run into and to apologize. But as the words were about to come out of her mouth, she realized it was the trucker she had angered yesterday.

"No fricking way. It's you again," the trucker said, frowning at her.

"I'm sorry. I truly apologize." She saw the coffee cup in his hand. "I'll buy you another—"

"Keep your damned money. Just stay away from me," he said, walking to the counter.

Pacie saw him talking to the cashier and then point back at her. She picked up her phone and drink—thankfully in a plastic bottle—as someone walked into a back room and returned with a mop.

"Sorry for the trouble," Pacie said.

"It's no big deal," the young man said. "Just watch your step on the wet floor."

Pacie continued to stand there until the trucker walked out the door.

"That was the truck driver, Greg Gumby from yesterday," Irma said, following Pacie to the counter. "Of all the people to run into."

"No kidding."

They paid for their drinks and walked outside. Greg's truck was pulling out of the lot. When they got back to the SUV, Irma poured a bottle of water into the dish she sat on the ground for Mr. Dibble.

"What did that email say?" Irma asked, standing at the open car door.

"I don't know," Pacie said as she climbed into the driver's seat. "I'll check it right now."

"It says, thank you for notifying us of the unusual hornets you have experienced in Black Water. We have forwarded your picture and message to the appropriate authorities." Pacie looked the email up and down. "That's it."

"They don't seem too worried," Irma said. "I guess the mayor wasn't exaggerating about the messages he got being generic and not voicing a great concern."

Pacie put the phone back into her satchel. "Yeah, even with a picture of a ginormous bee. But I'm not surprised. Even if they did take it seriously, I doubt they would tell ordinary citizens like us—they're not very transparent. Keeping us in the dark is kind of how the government roles."

Irma nodded. She put the bowl and dog back in the car. "Are you ready to go to Oscar's?"

With the angry Greg Gumby out of sight, and hopefully going the opposite direction, Pacie drove to Oscar's Vermin Control. When they arrived, a couple of other cars were in the driveway.

"Oscar looks busy today," Irma said as she and Mr. Dibble got out of the car.

The three of them walked into the store. Oscar was tending to concerned customers.

"See," Pacie said, "it's not just us worried about the hornets."

When the customers left, Oscar walked up to them. "Is that the nest?"

Irma handed the baggie with a piece of comb to him. "That's what the chickens tore up."

He studied it a moment. "It's a yellowjacket's nest, not what we're looking for."

Irma took the bag of nest pieces that Oscar handed back to her. "They can be nasty insects."

"Sure, the females sting. But yellowjackets are also important predators of pest insects like flies and spiders that they cut in small pieces to feed their young. Most people don't know that."

"You're right," Irma said, throwing the baggie into a nearby trash can. "I didn't know that."

"The giant hornets are doing the same thing as the yellowjackets," Oscar said. "They're just trying to survive. But I believe the big guys could be dangerous to humans, and something needs to be done to stop them. Have you caught one yet?"

Pacie said they would keep checking the traps and that they visited Mayor Castleman to see if he would cancel the festival.

"The mayor is making a mistake. We need to stay on top of this." Oscar looked out the store's window. "I'll be damned. The reporter from the TV station just drove up."

Pacie turned and saw Janet Sato walk up to the door with cameraman Carlos Hernandez. "It's our chance to warn people to be cautious tomorrow."

Oscar opened the door for them. "Hi, come on inside."

"Thank you, Mr. Schattschneider," Janet said as she stepped inside. "Wow, it's my lucky day. Pacie and Irma, glad you're here. Would you folks mind answering a few questions about the bees in town for WBLA TV?"

"I think it's a good idea," Oscar said, checking the buttons on his flannel shirt that he had cut off the sleeves. He looked at Pacie and Irma. "How about you ladies?"

"I'd like to," Pacie said.

Janet glanced around the showroom. "There," she pointed. "Stand in front of the bee supplies."

The three of them, including Mr. Dibble, stood where directed.

Janet looked at the cameraman and began counting down. "I'm here at Oscar's Vermin Control with the owner Oscar Schattschneider and Black Water's sleuths, Pacie Rose and Irma Foster." Janet looked at Oscar. "Mr. Schattschneider, what can you tell us about the monstrous bees we've been seeing around town? Are they anything to worry about?"

The camera turned to Oscar, who suddenly looked afraid. He cleared his voice as if he were about to gag. "Yes, I'd be worried. These huge hornets are not native to Michigan. They're most likely a mutant of some sort, and as such, little is known about them. Officials have issued no warnings as of yet, but I'm issuing my own warning for the residents of Black Water." He cleared his throat again as if mucous was being produced to stop him from speaking. "Until we have more information, everyone should stay away from these big hornets. Don't approach them. Don't make loud noises. Don't think they're stupid.

And it would be a good idea to look around your home for any openings that they could enter through. Just like mice, they seem to be able to squeeze through small spaces."

"Sounds like good advice," Janet said. "Do you have a way to get rid of them?"

Oscar did not want to mention his formula he was working on because he did not want the Environmental Protection Agency to shut him down. Instead, he said, "I'm looking into that. A nontoxic wasp spray suited to these flying critters would do the trick." Oscar gave the camera a fleeting glance. "I only use safe pesticides. Always. For now, if you happen to capture one, call me and I'll come out and get it. It'll help with my research. Just call me at Oscar's Vermin Control."

"While you work on finding the best, *nontoxic*, wasp spray, do you have specific tips to help people get rid of them?"

Oscar ran his fingers through his stringy hair. "All the usual stuff. Hang wasp traps, spray nests with store-bought wasp spray, or use soap and water. You can even make homemade traps by using a two-liter pop bottle and juice. You can find instructions on my website, Oscar's Vermin Control dot com. And if all that fails, give me a call, I'd be happy to help you get rid of the vermin."

Janet turned to Pacie. "Do you have anything to add to that?"

"Oscar's advice is sound and should be followed," Pacie said. "I would add that residents should consider not attending Harborside Jamboree, also called InkyFest tomorrow, because the hornets could be attracted to the loud music."

"Everyone loves InkyFest. It'll be hard to keep people away." The reporter turned toward Irma. "The news snippets that you send to us, the newspaper, and post on your website, Black Water Sleuths, are invaluable. Is there anything else we should know that has not been said?"

Irma put a hand on her fanny pack as though about to pull out a cigarette. "These hornets have wiped out local honeybee hives. You might not be aware that one third of our crops are pollinated by them. They also make honey, among other things. We can't have them destroyed by those giant mutants. We've been in contact with the Department of Agriculture, as well as Mayor Castleman. We'll keep you updated."

"Are you thinking the big bees will kill all the honeybees?"

"I don't know," Irma said. "But if they grow in number, it could be possible."

"That's alarming," Janet said, turning toward the camera. "This is Janet Sato reporting from Oscar's Vermin Control. Stay tuned for further news."

Carlos lowered his camera. "I'm going to get one— maybe a dozen—of those wasp traps and spray. Might as well be prepared."

While Oscar assisted Janet and Carlos, Pacie and Irma walked outside. The sable and white colored collie that had been lying under a maple tree meandered up to them. Pacie kneeled and petted the pooch; she could tell it was old by the way it moved like a senior citizen. She looked at the name tag on the collar. "Sadie," she read. "How are you, Sadie?"

Mr. Dibble walked up to Sadie and sniffed her, as if assessing if she were friend or foe. Or to simply say hello.

"He's been around Sadie before, hasn't he?" Pacie asked as she stood.

"Yeah, they're good friends. We visit Oscar every now and then."

"Have you ever considered dating Oscar?"

"Don't go there," Irma said, perturbed.

When they got to the SUV, Pacie reached inside and took a fuzzy peach from the orchard's bag and held it out for Irma. "Want one?"

"Aren't you going to make peach cobbler or something with those?" Irma said, taking the soft, round fruit.

"I don't know what I'm going to do with them." Pacie bit into a peach. Juice ran down her chin and dribbled on her shirt. "These are juicy. I guess we should be eating them before we get in the car."

"So what are we doing tomorrow?" Irma asked.

Pacie's cell phone dinged. "It's a text message from Bart. He says he called Johnny about his yacht being done and in the slip, but he wants to know if it's okay if he has your phone number." She looked at Irma. "Is it okay if I give Bart your number? He must want to see you."

Irma took a final bite of the juicy peach, then tossed the pit into nearby weeds. "If you give him my number, he'll be contacting me."

"That's kinda the point." Pacie smiled. "I have an idea. Maybe you can have him take you out on the water during the festival tomorrow. That way you can watch for hornet problems from the harbor."

Irma put Mr. Dibble in the backseat. "I suppose that's not a bad idea."

"I bet you'll have a great time while you're protecting the festival goers."

Irma did not answer while Pacie replied to Bart's message. "Be expecting a text or phone call. And *please* answer."

10

The Box

The windstorm that blew in from Lake Michigan kept Pacie awake most of the night. Powerful gusts of wind belted the old mansion as Pacie tried to sleep. The windows whistled and rattled, not only telling her that the weatherstripping likely needed changed and that something was loose, but also it could be a place where a sneaky hornet could enter the home. Scary moans emitted from the structure as if the wooden bones were bowing, about to reach their breaking point. She would have run out of the 1879 British Palladian-style mansion and drove to Johnny's, but the old gal managed to survive past atmospheric disturbances from severe thunderstorms with tornadoes during the spring and summer, to violent winter blizzards. Even so, the fact remained that as the decades passed, buildings can weaken, especially since she did a lot of the property maintenance herself.

Morning brought the realization that today was the day of the festival. Pacie was thinking about how she would plan the day. First, get the mail, something she had not done in a few days. Then call Johnny and see when he would be done working for the day. And, of course, see if Irma was going to spend time with Bart out on the water.

Pacie checked the news to see if anything horrific had happened during the night. Other than the powerful windstorm that caused scattered electrical outages, there were no swarms of hornets or injuries reported. The mayor would keep the festival on schedule.

The air was damp when Pacie stepped outside. She walked down the north path of the circular driveway. The estate was in worse shape than the mansion. There were once four magnificent gardens on the east side of the house. The garden to the south of the bowling green had symmetrical planting beds divided by wide pathways. Fruit trees were once skillfully pruned to grow flat against supports while dwarf boxwood bordered the beds.

The greenhouse used to grow lemons, limes, and oranges, but now only kept seedlings and ailing plants from old.

The kitchen garden to the north of the flat lawn was the main bed that Pacie maintained. Tomatoes, green peppers, cucumbers, and other common vegetables produced enough to can and freeze as well as give away.

The botanical garden, once used to grow plants from around the world to test and see if they would survive Michigan winters, was now a hodgepodge of interesting vegetation, now growing wild.

Old-fashioned apples, pears, cherries, peaches, and apricots still grew in the fruit garden, yet produced few quality crops. All Pacie did these days was mow around the trees, not bothering with sprays or pruning. The peaches from Handy's Orchard were far superior to hers.

Between the several acres of land and the three-story mansion, it was all Pacie could do to care for the ancestral grounds. While she was healthy, and had Johnny's help, she could keep the estate from looking like an abandoned manor, ripe for inviting looters and trespassers who filmed such things and posted online.

Damp gravel crunched under Pacie's sneakers as she passed the north garden. She would pick some vegetables on her way back from checking the mail.

The long grassy stretch between the connecting driveways—once used for lawn bowling and croquet—needed mowed, but it would have to wait until the hornet threat was taken care of; she did not want to make the pests angry by the sound of the mower's engine. Maybe the wind blew them away. She smiled at the improbable thought.

Small branches and other debris lay scattered about. She would pick them up later when she had more time.

As Pacie neared the road, she heard the noisy exhaust of the mail truck approaching. She noticed pieces of weathered white cardboard in the ditch, so she picked them up along with pages of a newspaper to clean up litter that the storm's wind had blown there. She held it up to see what the packaging said.

"Live queen bees?"

The mailman drove up and handed Pacie a couple of letters from the open door of the delivery truck. "Cleaning up trash that got blown around last night?"

"Hi, Lucy." Pacie held up the side of the cardboard—with a government address label smeared by rain and faded by sunlight—for Lucille to look at. "I wonder where this came from. Looks like there were bees inside."

The mailman's eyes widened. "Let me see it."

Pacie handed it to her.

"This looks like my bee package from a couple of months ago. It fell from my truck and got run over by some asshole trucker who kept tailgating and blowing his horn at me. I saw it get torn to shreds." She handed it back. "Don't worry; honeybees are the only bees we transport. Nothing dangerous."

"Why would the government be sending bees through the mail?"

Lucille shrugged, then changed the subject. "Are you going to the festival?"

Pacie nodded as she pondered the thought of where the bees went. Were they killed by the impact of the truck or released into Black Water? "Yeah, I'll be there. How about you?"

"Wouldn't miss it for the world. Well, I gotta go. Have a great day."

As Lucille drove off, Pacie walked along the ditch, looking for more pieces of the shredded box that—with any luck—could tell her more about what had been inside.

Pacie jumped when a harmless garter snake slithered away—it looked like no lady's garter to her. She almost gave up looking when a piece of paper near where the yellow striped snake had gone caught her attention. She cautiously walked up to it, not wanting to step on the reptile. She picked it up and walked back to the safety of the driveway.

The paper had writing on it, but it was faded and smeared from being wet. She would need to take it into the study and look at it under a magnifying glass.

After picking a handful of tomatoes and pulling a bunch of radishes, she went into the kitchen, where she threw the newspaper pages into the trash and laid the vegetables on the counter near the sink. Then she went into the study and laid the address information on her desk. She opened a couple of drawers until she found the magnifying glass she was looking for, then turned on the desk lamp.

She looked over the letters and numbers stamped on the cardboard pieces and on the address label. She was not sure she could decipher anything, but the one word that stood out was GOVERNMENT.

"I'll bet the giant hornets that are raising havoc around town were originally inside this box, and they're not honeybees," Pacie said aloud. "And the government has something to do with it. I've got to show Oscar."

Pacie was about to call him, then thought she had better check her wasp trap first and see if it had caught anything. She went across the central passage to the little parlor and looked at the wasp nest through the window. To her horror, it was moving. Something was partially stuck inside. She took her phone from her back pocket and took a picture, then sent it with a text message to Oscar.

Moments later, she received a phone call.

"Pacie, it's Oscar. Don't touch the trap. I'll be right over."

"I won't, and I found something that might be of interest to you."

"On my way."

Pacie inched her way to the window to get a closer look at the trapped hornet. She could not tell if it was Auntie Bee, but no matter, she had caught the sample that Oscar needed for his formula.

While she waited for Oscar to arrive, she called Johnny.

"I've found some interesting hornet info," she said.

"You should stay away from those damned things. I don't want to be visiting you in the hospital."

"Don't worry, I'm careful."

"I only half believe that." He paused. "What time do the bands start playing?"

"I think around four. Will you be done working at that time?"

"It's been busy here. It depends on if things slow down. I'll let you know what time I'm picking you up."

"Are we going out on the yacht?"

"That's my plan. I was thinking we could watch the bands play from the harbor—should be fun."

"I can't wait. Irma might be out on the water, too."

Johnny paused, then said, "Do you mean she's coming with us?"

"Well, maybe, but what I meant was that she might be with Bart, the harbormaster; out on his boat."

"Have you been playing matchmaker?"

"Only a little." Pacie could hear people chattering in the background.

"Hey, babe, I have to tend to customers. I'll talk to you later."

"Love you."

"Love you, too."

No sooner had Pacie checked the mail—the electric bill and an ad for a new pizza parlor in town—and washed the vegetables she had picked, than Oscar was knocking on the door.

"Hi, Oscar, come on in." Pacie motioned for him to step inside. "Glad you drove out here. I didn't really want to put that thing in my car."

With a cage and gloves in hand, he followed her out the lakeside door. "Oh, my. It looks like a bird got caught in there."

Pacie stood back as Oscar walked up to the trap.

"It was moving earlier. Is it dead?" Pacie asked.

"I'll tell you in a minute." Oscar sat down the cage and put on his gloves. "It looks like it suffocated in the liquid. I'm going to take the trap and all back to the shop. I want to cut this thing out without damaging it."

Pacie held up her phone and snapped a picture of Oscar and the trapped hornet before he secured it in the cage.

"I can't believe what I'm seeing." Oscar held the cage up, slowly turning it around to get a better look at the creature inside. "This is definitely a mutated hornet of some sort. I'll examine it back at the shop and let you know what I find."

"I can't wait to hear what you come up with." Pacie walked up to the trap, wanting to see if it was Auntie Bee, but she could not tell because of the way it had forced itself into the snare. "How did it manage to get inside the trap like that?"

"It reminds me of a pesky rat." Oscar took off his well-worn Detroit Lions baseball cap and wiped his forehead with the side of his arm before replacing it. "I've never seen anything like it. These things are powerful."

"That's scary."

"I'm gobsmacked. Things like this don't just happen out in nature. Something has helped them along."

"You mean like it was genetically modified by a lab?"

"Can't think of any other way these things could've grown like this." Oscar stared at the freak of nature. "By the way, that picture you sent me of the hornet outside Sam's was a queen."

"How could you tell?"

Oscar sat the cage on an Adirondack chair and fished his old flip phone from a pocket. "Look here," he pointed with a crooked finger to the hornet's back. "See that white dot?"

Pacie looked closely. "Oh yeah, I thought that was just part of its normal colors."

"It's a queen bee marking that's been painted on. There's a different color depending on the year. Since this one is white, she was marked last year. Queens only live around five years."

"Is this one a queen? The one in the trap?"

"I don't see a mark, but I'll know more when I get it out."

"So is this going to help you make a pesticide that will get rid of them?"

"I'm hoping it will." Oscar did not sound hopeful. "I just need to make sure it doesn't kill beneficial bees like honeybees and bumblebees. If I need to take care of 'em, I have to coax the fellows into a box hive and take them to a beekeeper."

"Sounds like it's going to take a long time."

Oscar shrugged. "Have you seen any more of these?"

"Irma hasn't told me if she caught one, but she probably hasn't been outside to check the trap."

"Let me know right away if she catches one. If we can nab the queen, then the colony will more than likely die if they can't find a replacement."

"If there's only one queen."

"There better be only one." Oscar picked up the cage and headed toward the door.

"Before you go, I need to show you something. Come with me to the study."

Oscar followed her to the desk where the faded papers lay under the light.

"When I walked down to get the mail, I found these lying in the ditch. The wind must've blown them there. They're pieces of a cardboard box. One has an address label that I can't read. Take a look and let me know what you think."

Oscar sat at the desk and picked up the piece that had LIVE QUEEN BEES printed on it. "A local beekeeper could've ordered a queen for a colony that recently lost one."

"But is says bees, plural."

"Queens are usually shipped with several, I think around eight, worker attendant bees."

"Look at the other paper." Pacie pointed toward the magnifying glass. "You might need that to read it."

Oscar picked up the lens and studied the faded words. "This is hard to make out, but I can for sure read GOVERNMENT. It looks like it's in both the mailing and return addresses."

"I saw that, too, but couldn't read anything else."

He looked up at Pacie, standing next to him. "I don't want to sound like a conspiracy theorist, but I'm gonna. It looks like it was on its way to a shadow government agency, but where?"

"It had to be headed to Black Water because our wonderful mail lady, Lucy, remembered her *bee package* and that somehow it fell off the truck a couple of months ago and then got run over by a semi and torn to shreds."

"You know this for sure?"

"Pretty sure. I picked it up and talked to her about it while she was delivering the mail today."

Oscar looked back down at the blanched paper. "There's no logical place in town it could've been headed to. The only government offices I know are downtown, but I'm sure our good ol' mayor doesn't handle bees."

"Maybe the college requested them."

Oscar leaned back in the chair and crossed his arms. "But it still makes no sense. Who in their right mind would order these danged giants we're currently dealing with?

No beekeeper I know. And they don't look like pollinators, so I don't know what they'd be good for."

"That is the question." Pacie leaned against the desk. "Lucille said only honeybees can be sent through the mail."

"These are no honeybees." Oscar wiped the spit from around his mouth. "Let's think about this."

"Okay. So what are you thinking?"

"If these hornets are what was in the box, and they escaped two months ago, like you said the mailman said, then they would've made a nest. The typical hornet usually makes their nests underground or in a cavity of some sort, like in a tree or building."

"Have any nests been found?"

"Not yet. But to continue my timeline, when the queen lays eggs, they'll hatch in a few days. Then they'll turn into ugly grub type things. Anyway, from egg to adult takes only around three weeks. Time—"

"Time for there to be more of these big bugs," Pacie interrupted.

Oscar looked up at her. "There very well could be. We need to find the nest and hope my formula works."

"Find the nest." Pacie shook her head. "How are we going to do that?"

"Well," Oscar began, "if they're in the ground, you'll find a hole that could be bigger than a walnut, going down over a foot or so. But these things," Oscar pointed to the cage, "would dig holes the size of an apple, hell, a grapefruit. And who knows how deep."

"A hole that size would be easy to spot," Pacie said.

"They could also find a cozy spot in a building. You have a lot of house here, and I'm sure there're cracks, vents, chimneys, and things like that. They could easily squeeze in through and nest. And since you actually caught one of those things, you'd best be careful and look around. I can do it for you if you like."

Oscar's cellphone rang. It was someone who spotted one of the giant hornets.

"You have a lot to do, tending to customers, examining this hornet, and working on a pesticide. I'll check things over myself and if I find anything suspicious, I'll call you."

"All righty then. But if you find anything, stay away from it. Barricade the area if you can."

"I will."

Oscar leaned forward and put his elbows on the desk. "Did you see the stinger on that thing?"

"I didn't look that close."

"It has to be as long as my thumb. If someone got stung on the chest, it would poke all the way through to the heart."

Oscar had to be exaggerating. But the fact that these hornets even existed made what he was saying to be a probability. "That would kill someone."

"Yup. Kill 'em dead as a doornail. Like getting stung by a small ice pick."

"Do you have to be so graphic?"

"Sorry. Just thinkin'." Oscar stood up. "I gotta be goin'. It's gonna take me some time to get this thing checked out. And I don't think time is on our side." He picked up the cage. "Maybe you could send these here papers to your cuz and have her scan them into the computer and see if she can run her magic on them and figure out what the rest of this says."

"That's a good idea. If anyone can figure it out, she can."

"Let me know if she has a bee in her trap."

"I will. I'll call her now."

Pacie walked outside with Oscar and sat down on the steps as he walked to his outdated van—rusted fenders, faded paint, and rear barn doors that he had to yank on a couple of times to get to open. She watched him put the caged deformity into the back and waved goodbye as she dialed Irma.

As soon as Irma answered, Pacie said, "You won't believe what just happened."

11

Calls

"What happened? You found a way to get rid of the hornets?" Irma asked.

"No, but we're getting closer. I caught one of those bees."

"I can't believe it. What does it look like? Have you called Oscar?"

"Oscar was just here. He's taking it back to his shop to do whatever it is he's going to do with it. As far as what it looked like, well, it looked like a cross between a wasp and a bird. It's absolutely terrifying. And get this, Oscar said the stinger was as long as his thumb. I took a picture, from a distance, of course."

"Send it to me," Irma said. "This is shaping up to be a real disaster. There should be some kind of warning or a biological alert on Black Water."

"Put a warning up on our website."

"I will."

"Have you checked your trap lately?"

"No, I haven't. I'll walk out there right now."

Sounds of movement and a door opening and closing suggested that Irma was wasting no time going outside and checking the tree where the bait hung.

The stair steps creaked with each one of Irma's footfalls. "I'm going outside now, and I can tell you it's busy around here. I bet Johnny's shop is getting a lot of business today."

"I doubt he'll make it to the festival until later this afternoon." Pacie paused, then said, "Are you there yet?"

"I'm there now and there's nothing in it."

"That's good. If there was, I'd be afraid these pests were multiplying fast, and that it wasn't safe to go outside."

"I'm disappointed and relieved at the same time." Irma looked at the car-filled parking lot and people walking around without a care in the world. "These people don't have a clue. It's not safe outside."

"I'm going to call the college and see if Professor Beasley knows anything about these hornets."

"I doubt he would because he's the lead anthropology and archeology professor, not an entomologist. Besides, it's Saturday, and he's probably not in his office."

"I'm going to try, anyway. Maybe Aileen can get me in touch with someone who might know about them. She sometimes works half days on Saturdays."

"It's a long shot."

Pacie heard Irma walking back into the building. "There's something else. When I got the mail this morning, I found pieces of a broken package that once had bees in it."

Pacie went on to explain what she and Oscar had spoken about. "I'll send you pictures of the faded address labels, too. Maybe you can use software to figure out what they say."

"I'll check it out," Irma said. "These hornets are so unusual maybe they can't reproduce."

"According to what Oscar tole me," Pacie said. "The bee package could've contained nine bees, the queen, and eight attendants. So it's one down and eight to go."

"Maybe we can set traps around town and catch the rest of them." Irma said. A door closed. "I'm back inside now. But people could die before we catch them all. We need to find the nest."

"Right. I'm going to call Aileen and go from there."

"I'll post the alert on our site and contact the stations and let them know what we've found out so far."

"Sounds good."

"Oh, wait, before you go. I almost forgot to tell you that I talked to Bart."

Pacie smiled. "Yeah?"

"Yeah. We're going to watch the bands from his boat in the harbor."

"I'm excited for you. I was afraid you would chicken out and not talk to him."

Irma laughed. "Me too. But then I thought, why not? It could be something fun to do. I'm sure you get tired of hanging out with me all the time."

"Never. Maybe Johnny and I will see you and Bart later today."

"I'll be looking for you."

Pacie looked at her watch. "It's almost one. I want to call Aileen before she leaves. I'll talk to you later."

The phone rang several times before it was answered. "Professor Beasley's office. How may I help you?"

Pacie recognized the southern accent. "Hi, Aileen, it's Pacie Rose. Do you have a minute?"

"For you, always. What's up? Need information on the unknown coin that was found in Ireland?"

"That sounds way more interesting than bees, but I was wondering if Professor Beasley has any knowledge about the hornets around town. The giant mutants. Anything that could help me, like did anyone at the college order them for study, or something like that?"

"The professor and I talked about it yesterday because of what we've seen on the news, and your website, but he doesn't know much more than I do. I think he and his wife were going to the festival; maybe you can catch him over there."

"Yeah, maybe." Pacie rubbed the back of her neck. "I know I'm asking a lot, but is there anyone at the college who would know anything about them?"

"Maybe someone in the Department of Entomology could help. Gary, he's a graduate student, might still be there. I saw him earlier when I was stretching my legs. I retain water and need to walk around every now and then. When the professor's not in his office, I put my feet up on the desk. That's what they say to do; raise your feet so they're above the level of the heart." She winced as if in pain. "The lab is on the second floor, room two ten. If you ever need to go there, be prepared, because I think he studies the bugs that grow inside dead bodies; things like disgusting maggots."

"That sounds gross."

"It is," Aileen said. "I'll transfer the call now. And you take care."

Pacie remembered noticing Aileen's compression socks the last time she and Irma had visited the professor. "Sure, that'd be great. And you take care, too."

The line clicked. After three buzzes, someone answered.

A nonchalant voice said, "Gary."

"Hi, Gary. I apologize for bothering you, but my name is Pacie Rose, and I was wondering if you could help me with the hornet problem we have in town."

"I know you. Aren't you the one who investigates cryptids, like Bigfoot and the Lake Eerie monster?"

"That would be me."

"I'd be happy to help. What do you need? I don't know much about cryptids, but I do know a lot about insects, obviously."

"As I'm sure you know, we have strange hornets flying around town. I was wondering if you or someone else ordered them."

Gary laughed. "No, but they would be interesting to study. Why do you think we ordered them?"

Pacie explained the destroyed box, escaped bees, and having caught one. "Oscar has the hornet right now."

Gary was excited. "Send me his contact information; I want to go over there. Did he take it to his shop?"

"As far as I know, he did. I'll send him a text so he knows you're coming out."

"Why does the exterminator want the hornet?"

"He wants to make a pesticide that'll stop them."

"Maybe I can help him come up with another solution. I hate to see something toxic sprayed around town."

"Oscar said he's making something safe. I believe him."

"No matter, I'd love to dissect it. I assume it's dead."

"I think it suffocated in the trap."

"Okay. Well, I still have work to finish up here; I don't know how long it'll take. I'm seeing how different poisons—arsenic, belladonna, strychnine—affect arthropods on a decomposing body when exposed to extreme heat, moisture, and low voltage electricity."

"I'm glad somebody likes to do that kind of work." Pacie chuckled, then said, "Can you check around and see if someone else had the government send those hornets here? And find out why."

"I will."

Pacie thanked Gary for his help, even though she learned nothing new, other than, as far as Gary knew, no one at the college requested the hornets. She sent a text to Oscar about a grad student maybe showing up and then sent Gary the contact information he wanted.

It was one-fifteen. Pacie knew Johnny would not be closing the shop this early, so now was the time to go through the mansion, searching for hornets and Auntie Bee.

12

Irma & Bart

Irma put one last curl in her short gray hair and unplugged the curling iron as the cuckoo clock announced the three o'clock hour. She applied the hairspray a little too heavily because there would be wind in the harbor, and she wanted her hair to stay in place. Stiff to the touch, yes, but it was highly unlikely that Bart would touch it.

She smiled at herself in the mirror as she smoothed the front of her three-quarter length sleeved blouse, lying loosely over her elastic waist slacks. The colorful geometric patterns of her shirt were eye-catching, maybe too much of an attention-getter. It had been a while since she last dressed up. As best as she could recall, the last time would have been when she, Pacie, and Johnny went to a beachside wedding last year.

It would not hurt if she lost a few pounds, but at least Bart did not ask her to bring a swimsuit. Thank God for small favors.

Nervous and on the verge of perspiring, her smile faded. Why was she doing this? She would be perfectly happy staying home and watching a good movie. Yet that would be depressing because while everyone else was out having fun, she would be alone with no one to talk to, except for her constant companion, Mr. Dibble.

The knock at the door made Irma jump. One last glance in the mirror. She drew in a deep breath to calm her nerves.

Mr. Dibble watched her from the couch.

"Stay there," she whispered to him.

Irma opened the door to find the rather handsome harbormaster. Pacie thought he looked like Popeye, but not her—well maybe he did a little. His thin silver hair was combed back, and he did not have a toothpick between his lips, nor the sailor cap on his head.

"Come in, Bart." Irma motioned for him to step inside.

He gave a nod and stepped over the threshold. "You have a nice place. It looks very . . . homey."

"Thank you. I spend a lot of time here." What a stupid answer. Obviously she spends a lot of time there, it's where she lives.

Mr. Dibble jumped off the couch.

"Oh, you have a dog. What's his name?"

"Mr. Dibble."

"He's acting like he's coming with us."

Irma picked up her purse from the counter. "He usually goes everywhere I go."

Bart looked at Irma, who was staring at him. "Ah, I suppose he can come along." He looked back at the dog, who was also watching him. "The more, the merrier."

"Thank you, Bart. He's a good dog, really he is."

"No doubt he is." Bart gave Mr. Dibble a pat on the head. "Are you ready to go out on the water?"

"I am." Irma was about to pick up her backpack, then decided against it. She was so used to carrying it with her, along with the fanny pack, that she felt naked without them.

Bart watched Irma reach for the pack and then change her mind. "Did you want to bring those? There's room on the yacht, if you do."

"I'm just in the habit of taking them with me when I go with Pacie. We do a lot of investigations, you know."

"Yes, I know. What I don't know is how you do it. You must be very brave."

No one had ever called her brave before. No, that's not true; it does come up on news reports every now and then. Part of her wanted to take the equipment because if they were attacked by hornets, she would have her wasp spray and her camera to record the whole thing. But asking Bart to take a dog with them on a first date was already asking a lot. Besides, she did not want to look . . . strange. "I can leave them here."

Irma locked the apartment door, then it was down the creaky old steps with Bart and Mr. Dibble right behind her. When they reached the parking lot, Irma looked around trying to determine which of the several parked cars would be his. She began walking to a large pickup truck she thought he would use to move boats around.

"This way," Bart said, walking up to a beige Ford Mustang.

"Nice car." Irma said as Bart opened the car's passenger door for her. It was the last car she expected someone who was in charge of a harbor to be driving. "I haven't been in a car like this in a long time."

Mr. Dibble shot into the backseat.

"It's a nineteen sixty-six Ford Mustang Coupe. Or pony car, if you like. I take it to car shows and drive it on special occasions."

Irma smiled as she sat on the blue vinyl seat. Was she a special occasion? She looked back at Mr. Dibble as Bart walked around to the driver's door. "I should've brought his doggy blanket. I can go get it."

Bart climbed inside, fastened his seatbelt, then started the car. "He's fine. Next time we'll bring his blanket."

Next time? Was Bart planning on seeing her again? Why not? She was not a bad person, just a bit of a loner.

They drove through the parking lot toward the marina. "I don't know if you're hungry, but I have food for us to eat later on the boat. We'll anchor so that we can get a good view of the festival and bands, and then we can dig in."

Irma was beginning to feel like she made the right decision to go out with Bart. Even so, she still felt awkward. Maybe she would disappoint him. After all, Biff dumped her, but that was a long time ago.

Bart slowed the car to allow pedestrians to cross the busy road. "Your dog is well-behaved. He's lying there like a good boy."

Irma glanced back at Mr. Dibble. His head was resting on his paws as if he were going to doze off, but his big brown eyes looked at her and then at Bart. "He is special. I don't know what I'd do without him."

Black Water buzzed with activity. Crowded sidewalks bustled with people carrying shopping bags. Eateries and outdoor seating were bursting at the seams. Irma was glad they would be out on the water and not packed like sardines along the harbor shore.

They crossed the drawbridge over Inky River and drove into the marina.

Bart pulled into a gated area. "I don't want anyone to slam a car door into my Mustang."

"I don't blame you," Irma said as she and Mr. Dibble climbed out of the car. "I forgot to bring a leash."

"Don't worry about it," Bart said, walking up to Irma. "He's gonna be trapped on a boat, not running around like a stray dog."

Irma appreciated Bart's easygoing nature. Not like Biff, who would tell her to lose weight and dress in nicer clothes. You're gonna be no trophy wife, he would say. Of course not, she would reply. You're not an old guy with a younger woman. Then, as his anger grew, he would say, you know what I mean. Like clockwork, Biff would then walk away, leaving her to wonder why she even stayed with him. And why did he stay with her? He didn't.

"Royal Fortune is ready to go. She's just waiting for us."

Even with fair weather and a mild breeze, halyards still managed to clank against masts. Water lapped and seagulls cried. Across the harbor, the festival was in full swing as it prepared for the bands soon to play.

As they walked to the docks, Irma tried to guess which boat was his. She was wrong about the type of vehicle he drove, so her first thought of it being the biggest one—he was the harbormaster, after all—would surely be wrong.

Then she saw it, a Jolly Roger pirate flag. By far, the largest flag on the sailing yacht was the Stars and Stripes, flown on a long, angled staff pole at the stern of the boat. But flying from the port spreader was a flag that said Harbor Master and beside it hung a black flag with a white skull and crossbones.

"Is that your boat?" Irma asked, pointing to the large yacht moored to the dock.

"What gave it away?"

"The flags made it rather obvious."

Bart laughed as they walked onto the dock.

Irma looked at the yacht in the next slip over. It looked old and worn, yet it was afloat. Then she noticed the name Zombie Refuge painted on the side of the bow. "Oh, that's Johnny's boat. Has he sailed it yet?"

"Not that I'm aware."

They walked down the dock and up to Royal Fortune.

"You have a very nice boat, Bart. How'd you come up with the name?"

"From my ancestor, Black Bart the Pirate. That's what he named his ships." Bart stepped onto the deck of the boat and held out his hand. "Grab hold of the standing rigging, and I'll help you onboard."

Irma grabbed the rigging and stepped onto the gunwale.

"Now step over the guard wire," Bart said, holding Irma to help her keep her balance.

"That wasn't so bad," she said as the boat rocked and she lost her balance, falling into Bart. "Oh, I'm so sorry. Guess it wasn't as easy as I thought."

Bart laughed as he held her close to his body. "Are you okay?"

It felt good to be near him. He smelled nice, like woody citrus, and his body felt more solid than she thought it would be. With his grip now loosened, she said, "I'm fine. Just need to get my sea legs."

"You'll get 'em." Bart motioned for Mr. Dibble to jump onboard. "Come on, boy."

Mr. Dibble leaped onboard, at first not knowing what to think about the moving floor below his feet.

"He'll get his sea legs, too." Bart laughed. "He's standing so stiff he looks like a yard statue."

"Hey, Bart," Tara said as she walked down the dock. "Need help with the lines?"

"Yeah, that'd be great." Bart looked at Tara and then at Irma. He pointed to bench seats around a table past the twin wheels. "Have a seat and we'll be underway."

Tara stood next to the boat. "You two should have a good time today. The weather is glorious. The only problem I see is finding a place to anchor. It looks pretty crowded over there."

"We'll find a spot," Bart said, standing at a wheel on the helm as he started the engine. "Did you want to come with us?"

Tara was all smiles. "Thanks for asking but I have other plans . . . like working. You know that."

"Just thought I'd ask," Bart said with his gravelly voice. "Don't want ya sayin' I never offered to take you out on the water." Bart took his sailor cap from a cabinet and placed it on his head. "You can release the lines."

Tara unhooked, then tossed the lines onto the boat. "Have a fun time. I gotta get back to work. I'll bet this is one of our most populated festivals."

"We'll see you later," Bart said, easing the boat away from the dock. Once clear, he pulled onboard the four fenders.

Irma waved at Tara, then said to Bart as he walked back to the helm. "How many of those hats do you have?"

"I have enough." Bart winked. "Hold on. We're not going far, but I don't want you to fall."

Irma held onto the table and called for Mr. Dibble to set next to her on the seat. Irma took her cellphone from her purse and searched for the festival's itinerary. Char's favorite band, Bad Credit, was the first to play. She should've asked Char what she would be wearing, that way she could better find her in the crowd.

Nearby boats tapped their horns and shouted greetings to Bart as he passed them. Irma could tell he was well-liked.

"I'll drop anchor here," Bart said, having found a spot where there was a good view of the stage.

The wind and waves were calm. A gentle rock lulled Mr. Dibble to sleep.

Bart sat on the other side of the pooch. "I have beer, iced tea, or bottled water. What's your pick?"

"What are you having?"

"Iced tea," he said. "I'd have a beer, but it's not a good look for the harbormaster to be drinking out on the water."

"Then why do you even have beer?"

"It's for when I won't be driving the boat. Just like a car, ya know."

"Of course," she said. "I'll have an iced tea with you."

"Come with me into the cabin and I'll show you around."

Irma followed him down a ladder and into the hull. There was more seating, a table, and a television. "This is just like an RV except instead of wheels, it has sails."

"You're right. It's exactly like that." He walked into the galley and took two bottles from the refrigerator next to the stove. He handed one to Irma. "The head is over there if you need to go to the bathroom."

"What's through there?" Irma said, pointing to a closed door.

"It's the stateroom." Bart opened the door, revealing a full-size bed and cabinets.

"I could almost live on this boat."

"Some people do," Bart said, watching Mr. Dibble look down at them from the top of the ladder. "It's a bluewater cruiser and designed for long trips. One thing I'd like to do, and haven't done yet, is sail from Black Water, through the Great Lakes, to the Atlantic Ocean. Just haven't had the time. But when I retire, I just might do it."

Irma looked at Bart's weathered skin and wrinkles. Retirement could not be that far away.

"Let's get up top," Bart said. "Your dog is waiting for us."

Irma looked at the steps and handrails. "Do you mind holding my tea? I think I'll need both hands to climb back to the top."

Bart took her drink and followed her back to the deck. He was about to set next to Irma, but Mr. Dibble beat him to the spot. "You have one devoted dog."

Irma patted Mr. Dibble's head. "Do you have any pets?"

Bart sat on the bench with Mr. Dibble between them. "I used to have a beautifully colored macaw that I trained to set on my shoulder."

Irma could tell that Bart loved his pirate ancestry. "Wasn't there a parrot in the book, Treasure Island? Was its name Captain Flint?"

"I don't know about that." Bart twisted off the cap of his tea. "But Crackerjack was a good ol' boy. He could even wave and play dead." He took a swallow. "I had him thirty years before he passed on. I miss him."

"I'm sorry." Irma pushed the thought of Mr. Dibble dying from her mind. She would worry about it when the day came.

"Hey, Bart," someone yelled from a nearby anchored boat. "How's it going?"

Bart waived. "Just gonna enjoy the show."

Soon other people were waving and shouting at Bart.

"Is there anyone you don't know?" Irma laughed.

"I get to know a lot of people, doing what I do."

Bart looked down at Mr. Dibble. "When we eat later, I'll figure out something for him. I made extra sandwiches."

Irma smiled. "He's okay right now."

It was a perfect day. The sun warmed her skin, and the air smelled of fresh rain. Bart's company was pleasant. She should be working on finding out more about the hornets and not lounging on a boat. But everything was peaceful. Hopefully, it would stay that way.

PART III
It's Here

13

Infiltration

Pacie put her cellphone in her back pocket and retrieved a flashlight from the butler's pantry.

"Now, where do I begin?" she said, looking around.

She doubted the kitchen and bathroom would have any places for the hornets to enter, since they were recent additions to the house. The most likely places would be the basement or the third floor.

Starting where she was at on the first floor, she checked around the windows and doors, and inside fireplaces. From the kitchen, through several rooms, to the two-story grand room—once used as a large dining area and ballroom—she saw nothing that caught her attention.

Some of the mansion's windows were original to the structure, while others—with cracked glass and warped frames—had been replaced by her and Patrick before his unexpected disappearance.

"Nothing here except cobwebs." Pacie ran a finger along the sill of one of the grand room's tall, arched palladium windows. She rubbed the brown dirt onto the pantleg of her jeans. "I've really gotten behind on my dusting. It's a good thing no one comes in here that often."

Pacie walked up the staircase to the second floor, first checking the blue room where Irma would occasionally stay. Then it was on to the Wolverine bedchamber, named after the Michigan Civil War brigade, which served under commander George Armstrong Custer during the Gettysburg Campaign. She continued through other bedrooms until ending in her suite. Many of the windows showed various degrees of wood rot and broken seals, likely the source of the old gal's moans and groans during storms.

"Okay," Pacie said as she ascended the steps to the third floor. "So far, so good. Or good enough."

The third floor had both bedrooms and storage rooms. A fine china closet with a large oval bull's eye window overlooked the mansion's driveway and bowling green. Pacie rarely went to the third floor, other than when she would climb the stairs in the winter for exercise.

With the cupola being the last area to check on the upper floor, she walked up the narrow stairway and sat in the small upholstered chair she had set to the side on the landing around the octagonal-shaped room. It was a beautiful place to read or to observe the grounds and the Great Water. Since the cupola was above the central staircase, not only did it let light flood down through the interior, but Pacie would open its windows on sweltering summer days, allowing for a much-needed draft through the mansion.

"I should come up here more often," Pacie said as she examined the window casings. Then she looked toward Black Water harbor and the festival. She could see boats dotted on the water and ants of people moving along the shore. "I hope Irma and Char are having fun and not running away from bees."

Most of the third-floor windows were originals and needed sills painted and cracked glass replaced, but none showed signs of any type of bee entry. She made a mental note of the windows that she, and Johnny, would need to fix.

"One place left to check," Pacie said, climbing down from the cupola, "the basement."

Like the third floor, the basement was one series of rooms she did not visit often. It was only when the water softener needed more salt that she—or Johnny—would venture down there.

Pacie walked down the staircase to the central passage. There were two ways to enter the basement; one from the outside, on the south side of the mansion, and the other underneath the central staircase.

With flashlight still in hand, she opened the door under the stairs. She felt for the light switch and descended the wooden steps to the brick cellar floor.

The basement extended the entire mansion, except for the new addition, and was comprised of a central passage with storage vaults, a cellar kitchen, and old living quarters with small egress windows.

Pacie looked inside the dark vaults that once stored foods such as turnips, butter, potatoes, pork, and beef, along with whiskey, wine, and brandy. The furnace room was fine, as was the dry well that once held ice or pork.

Pacie heard rumors of a secret basement, but she had not found it yet. Supposedly, the secret room had a getaway tunnel and ran down to the lake shore. Some said there was a lever to be pulled or something to be pushed to get a door to open, but as of yet, it was still a secret. Even along the lake shore, she saw no opening, but she reasoned it could have been covered by blowing sand long ago.

As Pacie walked to the south end of the passageway, toward the exterior double door, she stopped in her tracks. She could see light coming through the crack where the doors met. The mutant hornets could surely squeeze through it.

Distant humming set off her internal warning alarm — bees were in the basement. Even if they were ordinary bees, they were a threat to Pacie, because she did not have her EpiPen with her. Her best bet would be to turn around and move quickly and quietly to the exit. But before doing that, she shined the flashlight toward the far-off door. Large, odd looking, hornets were buzzing around what looked like a massive nest. These were the mutants. Time to go.

The humming stopped just as Pacie turned to leave. It was as if they noticed her. Then, to her horror, they shot toward her, just like in her dream.

14

Hold This for Me

Char and Renee danced to the rocking music of Bad Credit.

"This is the best festival ever," Char shouted over the loud music. She could feel the beat vibrating in her chest.

"Yep," Renee said, moving her head back and forth in a dizzying motion.

Char looked over at the harbor. "I wonder what boat Irma is on?"

"Don't ask me. I have no idea."

Char laughed. "I wasn't asking you. I guess I was talking to myself like a crazy person."

"You said it, not me."

They whooped and clapped when the song ended and the next one began.

"Can you hold this for me? I have to go to the bathroom," Char asked, handing Renee her paper cup of lemonade. "Don't move from this spot, or I'll never find you in a million years."

"Sure thing," Renee said, not taking her eyes off the band.

The porta potties were not far away. It was just a squeeze through the throng of bouncing people, and a short stroll down the sidewalk.

She waited in line outside the blue polyethylene outhouse. The aroma of grilled hamburgers from a nearby food cart made her smile and her stomach growl. Even a remote scream from someone in the crowd would not ruin the perfect day.

Char looked toward where the lake breeze was carrying the pleasing edible scent of food trucks and various carts and stands scattered nearby. She and Renee would grab something to eat during the next band intermission.

The door to the porta potty opened; it was her turn to enter the toilet.

After settling in and tolerating the stink of chemicals, screams of terror sent shivers down her spine. What was going on out there?

She quickly zipped her pants and peeked out the door. The line of people waiting to use the bathroom was gone, replaced by people running and yelling.

"Bees! Run!" Voices shouted as a frantic crowd ran past her.

"Oh my god. Grandma was right." Char closed the door and called 9-1-1. She got a recorded message saying the phone lines were busy, implying she was not the only person calling for help. It would not let her leave a message.

Char looked around the outhouse. There were no obvious holes for the bees to enter through, so it was probably safe to stay where she was. But what about her friend? She had to find Renee and run to the safety of their car, parked by the lighthouse beach.

The music stopped as a man forced his way into the potty, causing Char to fall back against the wall, almost into the hole. Then other people forced their way inside the crowded stall.

"I want out," Char pleaded as the bodies pinned her in an awkward position, causing her hand to touch gross wetness around the stool.

"Let her out and lock the door," a boisterous man shouted as he pushed people away from him.

Char struggled to escape the confines of the porta potty, and the intruders packed inside like sardines, leaving little room to move. An angry man pulled on Char's arm as she forced her way between the bodies, scraping her arms as the jerk shoved her out the door. She heard the door being latched behind her.

Char could not believe what she was seeing. It was like a nightmare as she ran to the band shell where she had left Renee. All she saw were bodies on the ground and people being carried away. It was chaos. A man ran into her, causing her to fall to the grassy ground, but she quickly got up for fear of being trampled.

"Renee! Where are you?"

With all the screaming and yelling, it was difficult to hear anything. When she could not find Renee, she figured she must have gone to the car.

Still fighting the unruly crowd, who was also running to the shelter of their vehicles, she kept calling for Renee. She looked over at the porta-potty she had been inside and saw a desperate gang banging on it, trying to get inside, until it was pushed over and onto its side. She cringed, thinking of the people inside now covered with biocides, blue dye, and bodily waste.

Now in the parking lot, people were driving like maniacs. A car brushed against her, blowing its horn as it sped away. If the bees did not kill her, the cars would.

Char spotted Renee's car; still parked in its spot. Hopefully, Renee was inside and waiting for her. But when she reached it, her friend was nowhere in sight.

What now? She had no key to the car.

She yelled Renee's name over and over, hoping she would hear it and know she was by the car and not taking shelter somewhere.

Char dialed her mom and dad, but could not get through to them. She was about to crawl under the car and hopefully out of sight of the bees when the car doors clicked, and Renee ran up.

"Quick, get inside."

They climbed inside, closed the doors, and looked at each other, so frightened they could not speak.

When a hornet the size of a house wren hovered in front of the passenger's window, they knew the end of the world had come.

15

Mow the Rows

Dale adjusted his headphones and baseball cap, then drove the small tractor and flail mower out of the barn. He would surprise Mr. Handy and mow the orchard so that he could get that hip operation that he needed.

He had mowed the orchard before, but he wanted to show initiative and prove that he could care for the orchard while Mr. Handy was busy doing other things.

Dale enjoyed working around the fruit trees and the chickens. Hell, even inside the country store. Someday he would own his own orchard and grow not only the typical apples, peaches, and corn like Mr. Handy sells, but also the less common pawpaw fruit.

The mow lines were straight and clean as he cut the tall weeds that shaded the cover crop. Dale was doing an impressive job. He would only mow a small section and then head back to the barn.

"Crazy bird," Dale said, swatting at the flying animal as it dive-bombed him.

Another hornet joined the first until there were a half dozen swarming around Dale. He stopped the tractor when one dove into the center of his back.

"What the heck?"

Dale removed his cap and swatted at them as he jumped off the tractor. Then he felt a sting, like a hot needle, puncture through the side of his neck. He pulled the hornet and its stinger out from the puncture wound. When he saw the blood on the two-inch stinger, he threw the vibrating pest away from him, but it returned to stab him again. And it did.

* * *

Mr. Handy heard sirens coming from town as he walked from the store to his farmhouse. Then he heard the tractor. He looked toward the orchard and the noise and saw Dale struggling against something next to the running tractor.

"What the hell?"

Knowing it would take him a while to reach Dale, he called 9-1-1. When he could not get through, he tried again, but to no avail.

He saw his wife hanging clothes on the clothesline. "Mother, call for an ambulance. Dale's in trouble."

Ida clipped a sheet with a clothespin and looked over to Mr. Handy, who was running toward the pickup truck. "What? I didn't hear you."

Mr. Handy did not answer as he climbed inside the old four-wheel-drive truck. When she looked toward the tractor and saw Dale in trouble, she knew she needed to call for help.

Mr. Handy drove into the orchard. As he approached the commotion, he saw giant hornets swarming Dale and the tractor. He laid on the horn until the mutants flew away. He jumped out of the truck and ran to Dale.

"Dale, you got to get up." Mr. Handy tugged on Dale, trying to get him to stand.

Dale got to his hands and knees and vomited. "I was stung by whatever those things were."

"Come on, we need to get you to the hospital."

Mr. Handy helped Dale into the cab of the truck, then sped toward the house where Ida was standing in the yard watching.

"I'm taking him to the emergency room." Mr. Handy slowed only enough to get the message to his wife. "Call his family. Let them know what's going on."

"What's going on? What happened?"

Mr. Handy kept driving, then shouted out the window to her, "Stay in the house. Don't go outside."

16

Bobbing

"You make a good sandwich," Irma said, dabbing her lips with a plain white napkin.

Bart adjusted his sailor cap. "Actually, cooking is one of my hobbies."

"Really?" Irma put her napkin and sandwich packing in the now empty paper lunch bag. "You're full of surprises."

"I am?"

"That's not a bad thing," Irma said. "Driving a Mustang and culinary skills wasn't what I had envisioned about you."

"So what did you envision?"

"I don't know. I guess it's just that I'm getting to know you."

"Are there any surprises that I need to know about you?"

Irma shook her head. "I don't think so. I'm a pretty average person, but Pacie might tell you otherwise."

"I know you're a Black Water sleuth with your cousin. And now I know that you have a dog. Is there anything else?"

"No, that's all there is about me."

"Irma," Bart said as he reached over Mr. Dibble and touched her hand. "I like you just the way you are. Even if surprises pop up along the way, I don't think that'll change anything."

Irma blushed. Was Bart going to kiss her?

But before the magical moment happened, screams soon replaced the festival's music.

"What's going on over there?" Bart stood and looked at the mass of festival goers running around in a disorderly mass. "Something's wrong."

"It's the hornets." Irma stood next to Bart. "Pacie and I were worried this was going to happen. We need to get somewhere safe."

"There's nothing we can do, short of calling 9-1-1. I'll get us back to the marina."

While Irma tried calling for help from her phone, Bart took to the helm and pushed a button to pull up the anchor.

"Hey, Bart," a man dressed in a French navy black and white horizontal striped Breton shirt yelled from a nearby sailboat. "What's happening onshore? Those people are running for their lives."

"I don't know, but it might have something to do with bees. I suggest getting somewhere safe."

"I think they're overreacting about some stupid bees," the man said, watching the stampede as if entertained.

"I can't reach anyone," Irma said, beginning to feel panicked.

"Did you at least get a hold of 9-1-1?"

"No, nothing."

Soon screams were coming from the boats closest to shore. Irma took a small pair of binoculars from her purse and looked at the people crying from nearby boats.

"Oh my god, it's the hornets."

"What is it about these bees that are upsetting everyone?"

Irma handed Bart the binoculars. "Look."

Bart held them to his eyes. "Those aren't hornets; they're birds of some sort."

"They're bird-sized hornets. And based on the people I see lying on the ground in front of the band shell, they're deadly."

"I need to help them," Bart said, navigating to the boats under attack. "You and Mr. Dibble, get inside the cabin. You'll be safe there."

"But you'll be attacked if you stay out here."

"If I get attacked, I'll be joining you in a hot second."

Irma tried to put Mr. Dibble through the cabin door but he refused to go; like a dog who loves water but hates baths, dragging his legs all the way.

"You shouldn't be out here," Bart said as he maneuvered close to the boats under attack. "Damn, those things are big and vicious."

Irma began thinking about how she could protect herself and Bart from being stung. "Do you have a fishnet?"

"Over there," he pointed.

Irma held the hand fishing net like a batter waiting for the pitch.

"Jump onboard," Bart shouted to the couple who were in a smaller boat with no access to shelter and clad in a bikini and tight Speedo swimming trunks.

Irma reached out and helped them over the rail. Right in front of her, a hornet swooped toward the woman, but Irma intercepted it with the rubber net bag. The hornet was strong and would soon fight its way out of the netting.

"Release it into the locker under the bench seat," Bart shouted to Irma as he maneuvered alongside the next boat. People were jumping over the side of their rigs and into the water. "Lower the swim platform so they can climb onboard."

Mr. Dibble leaped into the air and bit any hornet that came his way. He was having fun; he was on the hunt.

Irma snagged two of the hornets before they finally flew away. She scooped up the ones that Mr. Dibble had damaged and put them in the buzzing locker with the others. The man who was earlier making fun of people running from the bees was now dripping wet, having been one of the people who abandoned ship and had climbed onboard. He changed his tune as he sat on the bench seat to keep the hornets from escaping. Inside the box sounded like a game of vibrating ping-pong balls as the hornets that could fly thrust their bodies into the sides, looking for a way to escape.

"I think it's over," Bart said, holding the boat's position while other boats cleared out of the area. "Is anyone hurt?"

"Not that I know of," Irma said. She opened the cabin door where most people had retreated. "Is anyone hurt?"

"I think we're fine in here," a woman said, adjusting a towel she clenched over her swimsuit. "We're just scared."

"The bees are gone. You can come out if you want," Irma said.

"If they're gone," a man said, climbing out of the cabin, "I want to get back to Zephyr."

After thanking Bart and Irma, the rescued people returned to their boats and sped away.

"Time for us to get back to the marina," Bart said. He looked at the locker holding the agitated hornets. "What are we going to do with them?"

"I'll call Oscar the pest control guy, if I can get a call through. I'm sure he'll come and get them," Irma said. "In the meantime, we need to make sure they don't escape."

Bart reached into a helm compartment and brought out a padlock. He put it through the latch, leaving it unlocked. "This will keep them contained, at least for now."

"If they break out of there, we're all in trouble," Irma said.

Bart nodded. "You're right, but I don't think they can get out. It's a metal box."

"Sounds like they're putting dents in it."

Irma looked at the park where the festival had been, now surrounded by fire trucks and ambulances. Paramedics carried people out on stretchers through the panic that still ensued onshore while sirens wailed. Fortunately, she didn't see any hornets flying around.

Irma's call to Oscar went to voicemail. She left a message and called Charlotte.

"Irma, are you okay?" Char said.

"I'm fine. I'm out on the water with Bart right now. How are you? Where are you?"

"I'm okay. I'm with Renee in her car. We're trying to get out of the parking lot, but there's a traffic jam."

"Stay in the car and head home."

"That was the plan. What are you going to do?"

"We're heading back to the marina. Have you heard from your mom or anyone?"

"Mom and dad are at the house, but I haven't heard from grandma yet. That's not like her. She would've called and checked on me by now. Do you think she's hurt or something? She won't answer my call."

"I'm going to try her next. Call me if you need anything."

Irma at once called Pacie; all she got was the voicemail. Having gained her sea legs the hard way, she walked up to Bart at the helm. "I can't get a hold of Pacie. I think something's wrong."

"Where is she?"

"I'm assuming at her house, but I don't know for sure. I'll call Johnny."

Johnny answered on the first ring. "Irma. Is Pacie with you?"

"No, I was hoping she was with you."

"I haven't been able to get her on the phone. Do you know where she could be?"

"My guess is at the house. I'm at the marina and can't get over there. Can you check on her?"

"My store is packed with people fleeing the bees. A ton of them need medical attention, so I can't leave. I seem to be the only one who knows first aid." A woman in the background shouted that someone was not breathing. "Can you get over there and check on her? I gotta go."

As Bart swiftly pulled into the slip and began tying down the yacht, people ran up to him, telling him about the swarm of bees they had been fighting.

"Can you drive me to Pacie's?" Irma asked, knowing Bart had his hands full at the marina.

"I don't have time. I gotta keep things under control here. I might even have to go back out on the water." He fished the Mustang's keys from his pocket. "Can you drive a manual transmission?"

"Uh, it's been a while." Irma took the keys. "I'm not a very good driver, that's why I don't have a car."

"It's like riding a bike. Take the Mustang and be careful; those bees from hell could come back."

Irma nodded. "They probably will."

Irma and Mr. Dibble ran through the open gate to the Mustang and climbed inside. She put the key in the ignition and sat there a moment as Bart ran inside the marina.

"Let's see if I can remember how to do this," she said to Mr. Dibble.

One foot pressed the clutch pedal to the floor, and the other did the same with the brake. Irma turned the ignition, and the Mustang roared to life.

"Now the hard part."

17

Dark Room

There was no way she could make it out of the basement before they caught her. A nearby brick vault with a wide arched wooden door was her only option. She ran inside the room and used her body weight to close the door that had not been closed in decades.

There was no latch to secure the door on the inside, so she dug her heels into the dirt floor beneath the loose bricks and pressed her back against the damp wood, keeping pressure on it so that it would not open. She felt the hornets pushing on the door as if they were a team working together. She could even hear what sounded like a woodpecker pecking away at the dark wood, looking for ants and grubs, or signaling for help from others in its clan. The door was thick, at least a couple of inches. If she could keep it closed, there was no way they could break through. Or so she hoped, because she did not have her EpiPen with her.

Pacie looked into the dark, looking for any light leaking through cracks. There was none, but the basement lighting system was dim, so there would be little light seepage into the chamber.

At least she had her phone in her back pocket. She slipped it out and with pressure still against the door and called 9-1-1. When it did not connect, she noticed there was no cell signal in the room. She tried Johnny's number just in case it would work, but as expected, it did not connect.

All there was to do now was to wait for the hornets to go away or for someone to come to her rescue. Both would take a while.

The storage room was chilly, damp, dark, and scary. It was the old wine cellar. Dusty old bottles still lay in racks. If she were there a while, at least she would have something to drink, she said in jest.

The hornets were relentless in their efforts to reach her and cause harm. Why were they so determined? Hopefully, Oscar was coming up with some answers and solutions to this miscreation of nature.

Pacie slid her back down the door until she was setting on the cold dirt. She wondered if she could hear a car door close because she would begin yelling for help. But if she did that, not only would it attract more hornets to her location, but she would also bring Johnny or Irma into the hornets' nest, where they could be stung multiple times and die. The best thing to do would be to wait until she could hear the hornets no more and quietly sneak out of the room and back upstairs.

Right now, the flying insects were still trying to break through the decaying door. Hopefully, there were no soft and rotten spots that would be easy to penetrate. If there was, she would be doomed.

18

Inspection

A blue compact Kia was setting in the driveway under the shade of a maple tree when Oscar returned from a service call. He drove past it and parked near the shop's side door entrance. Oscar took his backpack sprayer from the rear of the van as he watched a big young guy squeeze out the door of the tiny car.

The obese man lumbered up to the van. "Are you Oscar?" Gary asked, extending a fleshy hand. "I'm Gary from the college. I called you earlier."

Oscar's bony fingers shook Gary's soft digits. "Good to meet you. I've been so busy I haven't had a chance to give the captured hornet a good lookin' over."

"I'd like to help you. Since I'm a grad student in the entomology lab, I can take the specimen back there if we need to."

Oscar walked through the side door, directly into his workshop. "I'm set up pretty well here, but it's good to know your lab is available if we need it."

"Where is it?" Gary glanced around the cluttered room. Papers, cans, cups, and various tools lay scattered over most of the work surfaces.

"I'll show you in a minute. I want to get this filled first." Oscar sat the sprayer on the floor near an elevated barrel with a spout and began refilling the sprayer's plastic tank. "But it's over there in the fridge if ya can't wait."

"Have you looked at it yet?" Gary asked as he plodded to where Oscar was pointing.

"Only to take it out of the trap that it was stuck in. I think it drowned itself. But then I started getting service calls and had to stop checkin' it out. It's been damned busy around here lately."

Gary opened the refrigerator door and saw what had to be the specimen setting on a blue-rimmed dinner plate. "Do you have disposable gloves?"

"Somewhere around here." Oscar ran out of the cumbersome gloves a long time ago.

"I have a box in my car. I'll be right back," Gary said.

Oscar finished filling the sprayer and returned it to his van. Gary followed him back inside the building and to the refrigerator. Oscar took the plated specimen to his worktable and turned on a bright light.

"Here," Gary said, handing Oscar a pair of plastic gloves.

Oscar hesitated a moment, then took the sure to hinder handwear. He did most of his work without them because the baggy things simply got in his way. But since he did not want to set off any safety alarms in Gary's head that might shut him down, he said a little ol' white lie.

"I ran out of these and just haven't had time to replace them."

Gary said nothing as he picked up the handheld magnifying glass on the table and began inspecting the hornet. He oohed and awed until he gasped.

"This is truly astonishing. I've seen nothing like it." Gary looked Oscar square in the eyes as if he had discovered gold. But instead of gold, it was as mind-blowing as an ancient demon relic. "This, whatever it is, has definitely been genetically modified. It even has what appears to be an artificial object mounted on it."

"Let me take a look before the phone rings." Oscar took the plate from Gary and slid it underneath the desktop magnifier. He flipped the lenses switch on and off a couple of times, jiggled the cord, and rapped at the mount until the light around the magnifier came on. He lowered it toward the specimen and turned the magnification knob. He studied the dead thing. "I'll be damned. If I didn't know better, I'd say it's been harnessed with a miniature camera."

"I've never seen or even heard of anything like this," Gary said. "What would be the reason for all this?"

Oscar looked at Gary over the top of his glasses. "Pacie thinks someone at the college might of ordered them."

"I don't know anything about that. Or why anyone would even want them." Gary paused, then said, "Actually, I wouldn't mind having it to study."

"Somebody wants it, and we have ta figure out who and why."

"I want to see it again," Gary said. "Why would a camera be on this . . . creature?"

Oscar stepped aside. "It's big brother. The box these freaks were inside came from our good ol' government. Irma's going to try and decipher the water-stained addresses."

"You actually found the box it came in?"

"Pacie found it shredded out by the road and apparently Lucille, our mail lady, remembered she lost it off the mail truck a couple of months back."

"This is truly disturbing." Gary shook his head. "But as far as the specimen before us, I'd say it's a cross between a Vespa mandarinia and a hummingbird."

"That's what I figured when I took it out of the trap. This creepy wasp has its beady little eyes on the front of its big head, and it doesn't have any dots oozing off its stripes."

"So we agree it's likely a cross between an Asian giant hornet and a hummingbird, probably an Anna's hummingbird."

Oscar rubbed his chin, covered in bristly whiskers. "Okay, that makes sense. If it's being used as a weapon of war, it can swarm troops and sting them to death. The camera, well, maybe they can be controlled by someone who sees where they're at and tells them what to do and where to go. So they can be danged precise in who they target. They have to be intelligent, or at least like drones that are programmed to do what they're told."

"An Anna's hummingbird can fly sixty miles per hour, hover, and dart this way and that," Gary said. "Like you hypothesize, it fits as far as being something that the enemy will have difficulty stopping."

"This combination makes them not only deadly, but easy for them to penetrate battlefields or to target a single person," Oscar said. "I think we're on to something."

"I think you're right."

"Ya, know," Oscar said. "That camera could be recording us right now, and if they are, then they know that we're on to them. This could get rather dangerous for us."

"I want to know why it's here, in Black Water. We don't have a military facility." Gary pulled a nearby stool up to the workspace and sat down. "I'd say the post office made a mistake, but if that was the case, then why wasn't your mail carrier surprised it was on her truck and send it back? It had to be coming to someone in town."

"I don't know but be careful on that stool." Oscar watched Gary rest a foot on a broken, wobbly barstool ring. "It's a secret operation. It's a clandestine intelligence operation. We need to get the camera off of it and put it where we can't be seen or heard."

"Before we do that," Gary said, taking the phone from his pocket. "Let's get some pictures."

After the two of them took pictures, the shop's phone began ringing.

Oscar took a small metal toolbox from a nearby shelf and sat it on the table. "While I'm out fighting these freaks, can you take that camera off and put it in this? I might not have time to do it myself."

"Not a problem," Gary said as he checked the pictures he had just taken. "My pictures aren't uploading to the cloud."

After answering the phone, Oscar walked back into the workshop. "There's a problem at the festival. People are being attacked by bees. Usually, I get calls on my cellphone but since they seem to be calling by landline, can you answer the shop phone for me while I'm gone?"

"What do I tell people?"

Oscar picked up an extra canister of the special hornet formula on which he was working. "Just take a message and don't make any promises."

"Will do."

Oscar tried to call Pacie to let her know what he had found with the captured hornet and that the festival was being swarmed, but got no answer. He tried Irma and could not get through either. "Cellphones aren't working."

"What? Call my phone."

Oscar called Gary as he walked to the side door. "I just called you."

"I didn't get it. The cell towers must be down," Gary said. "Plus, I still can't back up my photos to the cloud."

"Use the Wi-Fi," Oscar said, resting a hand on the doorknob. He did not want to leave until things were taken care of.

"What's your password?"

"Shit." Oscar sat the canister on the floor. "I'm going to send mine to print on the office printer. Bluetooth should be working."

Gary followed the sound of the printer. "It worked; your pictures came out."

Oscar logged on to his computer. "The Internet's down, too." He wrote the network password on a notepad. "I wrote the password down for ya. It's by the computer."

Oscar huffed as he walked back to the canister. "There ain't any storms so there's something else goin' on. Somethin' bad. If I didn't know better, I'd say the government is blacking us out."

"I might have to take this to the entomology lab at the college," Gary said.

"I don't really want that freak of nature to leave my workshop because I might never see it again," Oscar said as he opened the door. "But whatever you decide to do, just be sure to let me know. Leave me a handwritten note, with directions, even if the phones start working."

"I will. And be careful out there."

"Oh, don't you worry about that," Oscar said. "Can you set up a pheromone trap outside for me, over on the old apple tree? The stuff's over there," he pointed. "I figure that if we can catch the queen, we can lure the rest of them to us and stop them all in one fell swoop."

The phone rang.

"That call's on you, Gary. And can you keep Sadie inside with you?" Oscar called for Sadie, who was already walking up to him. "Come on, girl; get inside."

"I'll keep her safe," Gary said, walking to the front sales counter to answer the telephone.

19

Blocked

Gary answered the old wall phone but could not recall the name of Oscar's shop.

"Oscar's."

The caller said nothing at first, likely wondering if she had called the correct number. "Is this Oscar's Vermin Control?"

"It is. I apologize for the confusion, but Oscar is too busy to answer the phone. How can I help you?"

"My name's Marie and my house is being attacked by birds that look like bees." The woman spoke quickly with a voice that was rising to a panicked pitch. "I feel like I'm in that Alfred Hitchcock movie, The Birds. I live by the harbor, and I can tell you that the festival is being flooded with a flock of these ugly monsters. People are running for their lives. I—we need your help."

Gary knew this was a lame response to her request, but he said, "I don't know when he can get out to your house and help you, but I'll pass the message on to him. Leave me your name and address, along with your phone number. And don't go outside. Keep the house closed up, and you should be all right."

"I'll do the best I can." The woman did not sound convinced that this was the best course of action.

Then Gary realized that Marie was able to call the shop. "How'd you call here? I mean, what did you use?"

The woman explained that her cellphone was not working, so she had called on her landline telephone. She left both her landline and cell numbers with an urgent plea to get out there as fast as possible.

Gary hung up and called Oscar from the same phone, but it did not go through. "Must be phones work, but only landline to landline. Oscar did say this was a landline phone."

The shop's yellow corded phone hung on the wall behind the service desk. Most people he knew used cellphones, not landlines. He thought a moment, trying to figure out whom he could call to test his theory. "Of course, the college should have landlines."

The only number he could immediately recall was to the entomology lab.

But no sooner had Gary hung up the phone when a second call came in. He answered it. After getting a similar frantic plea for help, he gave the same response. He felt like Oscar's secretary, which was fine, but if the phone did not stop ringing, he would not be able to get to the college and do a more accurate assessment of the specimen.

Finally, the calls slowed until they stopped. It was either because the hornets had left the area or people thought the shop was closed. Now was the time to call the lab and hang the pheromone trap. From the wall phone, Gary dialed the entomology lab. It rang. And even though no one answered, he knew he had found a way to communicate.

He looked at his watch; it was six o'clock. Shadows grew long outside the shop as he hung the pheromone trap on an old apple tree and walked up to the front door. The sign hanging behind the glass said that the shop had closed an hour ago. He went inside and flipped the plastic sign over to CLOSED PLEASE CALL AGAIN, locked the latch, and left a message on a notepad by the computer that he was taking Sadie and the specimen to the college lab. He wrote the lab's phone number and asked Oscar to call him, explaining that only landline to landline calls worked.

Then he walked into the workshop as Sadie followed his every step throughout the shop as if she knew there was something dangerous going on.

Now was his time to leave. Gary tried Oscar's cellphone, but the call did not go through. He placed the specimen, now at room temperature, into a clear, small plastic trash bag he found on a shelf and secured it tightly. He opened the refrigerator and saw the freezer had an ice cube tray with a few frozen cubes that he could use to keep the hornet somewhat cold.

Beside the fridge was a metal-domed lunchbox. He unlatched it, and after recovering from the rancid smell of an old bologna sandwich, he emptied it and carefully placed the bagged specimen inside. He dumped the ice over it and closed it.

"I'll take the camera off at the lab. That'll be a whole lot easier than messing with it here." Gary picked up the toolbox and lunchpail and walked to the side door. Cautiously, he opened it and listened. He heard no buzzing and saw no movement, other than a few rustling leaves from what was surely just a breeze.

"Come on, Sadie. We're going for a ride."

The collie just stood there.

Gary walked past her and turned around. "Come on, girl." He slapped his thigh a few times as some type of signal, he supposed. But she was not leaving the building.

"Am I going to have to carry you?" He walked up to her and gave her a few nudges. "Come on, it's safe right now."

Sadie was beginning to back up. Gary sat the lunch and toolboxes on the ground and grunted as he bent over and lifted the dog. "You're heavy."

Gary was out of breath when he reached his Kia. He put Sadie down, opened the passenger door, and was forced to lift her into the seat. At least she was not fighting him, only dead weight.

Gary rushed to where he had left the specimen containers and plodded to the car. He closed and locked the doors. He put the lunchpail and toolbox in the backseat. Now to get to the college.

He decided to drive the back way to the lab to avoid traffic. Sadie had settled onto the seat beside him.

When he pulled up to a stop sign on the outskirts of Black Water, he had to wait for a long line of cars that appeared to be leaving town. He turned off his blinker, deciding he would be better off crossing the street and turning a block or two up.

Then he noticed people turning around and coming back. He was sure he had seen that red sedan and the potato chip delivery truck going the other way.

Now the traffic stopped, and no one was giving him room to cross. "What is going on?"

Sadie looked up at him as he mumbled. "I guess I'll turn around and use another road."

Gary backed up a few feet and cranked the wheel as he drove forward and then back again until he was going back the way he had come. He drove up to a dirt road and turned left, heading out of town.

"I can't believe I have to do this." He looked at his gas gauge; it was on an eighth of a tank. Enough to get to the college, but not if he had to drive tons of extra miles to get there.

The car rumbled down the dry gravel road as it kicked up dust behind it. He looked in the rearview mirror and saw a car gaining on him.

Then he saw flashing lights on the road ahead at the intersection. He slowed as he approached the blockade.

A police officer signaled for him to stop.

Gary rolled down his window. "What's going on, officer?"

Things did not look right. Gary was not an expert in law enforcement, but he had read enough crime novels to at least know the basics. The man before him was not from the local police department, nor a state trooper. The gold badge worn on the chest of his black uniform resembled that of the FBI, with a bald eagle at the top, a blindfolded Lady Justice in the middle with a scale and torch, and the words FEDERAL BUREAU OF INVESTIGATION, the letters U and S, and DEPARTMENT OF JUSTICE embossed on it.

As far as Gary could tell, it was an official FBI badge. But most special agents carried their badges in a billfold along with an identification card. Besides, FBI agents were more like Fox Mulder and Dana Scully of the X-Files, dressing in either a suit or casual clothing. Nothing, other than this man's badge, said FBI. Aside from lights on the cars and SUVs, there were no identifying signs of where they were from. Even the officers, if they were officers, looked as unmarked as the vehicles. He saw no verbiage, other than the intimidating man's badge standing by his car, that said if the blockade was being enforced by the Black Water Police Department, State Police, or CIA for that matter. But what he could identify was the soft bulletproof vests they wore and their well-equipped duty belts with a holstered handgun, radio, taser, handcuffs and other items that gave citizens, like himself, the message that they were not to be messed with. Even the dark sunglasses that they all wore added to their anonymity.

The officer, or more likely a special agent, gave him a stern look, as if Gary was going to give him a hard time.

"You need to turn around," the agent said.

"I'm trying to get to the college, but all the traffic is making it difficult," Gary said. "I thought that if I took the back roads around town that I could get over there."

"You can't get through here. You have to go back."

Then Gary heard a rustle from the backseat. Was it the hornet coming back to life inside the lunchpail? Gary began to perspire as both he and Sadie looked toward the backseat. If this was a secret FBI team, it was likely related to the specimen he had in the back. If they found it, they would probably arrest him and take him to a forced labor camp in Alaska, never to be seen again. This whole mutant hornet thing had to be top secret and could not be revealed to anyone.

"Uh. Probably a mouse," Gary lied. "I've had an infestation in my house, and you know how mice are; they can sneak into anything, especially when looking for food. I've set out traps and—"

"Step out of the car, please," the agent said.

"I'm kinda in a hurry."

The agent rested his hand on the holstered firearm. "I'm not asking you again. Step out of the vehicle."

Gary's hand shook with fear as he opened the door. He was about to step out when a car horn began blasting from behind him. He heard a man shouting that his wife was in labor.

The agent walked toward the car that was now trying to drive around Gary. He heard the driver ask if anyone could help him get his wife to the hospital. Instead of receiving help, a gang of agents surrounded the sedan.

This whole situation was wrong. Gary closed his door and turned around, the same thing everyone else was doing, and sped down the road. He looked in the rearview mirror when he heard gunshots.

"Shit. Shit. Shit."

20

Crack

Pacie crossed her arms to ward off the chill radiating from the basement floor and walls. She still heard the hornets on the other side of the door, but there seemed to be fewer of them. Nevertheless, it was not safe to leave the room.

Knowing that the hornets can squeeze through tiny cracks, she kicked loose bricks to the side and packed dirt around the base of the door. Granted, they surely could push away the dirt, but it could buy her some time. Time for what? A few seconds longer to wait to be stung and die.

She shined her phone's light around the cellar. Behind the wine racks, against the wall, was a sheet of plastic that was probably used as a vapor barrier. She pulled on it until a section came loose. The edges were damaged, so she tore it into ragged strips and began stuffing it between the door and frame. Again, another weak defense.

As far as Pacie saw it, the hornets needed to give up or someone had to come to her rescue. Right now, neither was happening.

With the cracks now stuffed, Pacie walked to the chamber's back wall, trying to figure out what else she could do to keep the insects from entering. She could think of nothing.

All she could do was wait. And pray.

21

Stuck

Now that an ambulance had finally arrived downtown, Johnny ran outside and up to a paramedic who was moving in fast motion. He told him that a woman was having difficulty breathing and needed immediate attention. That she was over there in his shop; he pointed.

The paramedic seemed to almost not hear him as he pulled a stretcher from the back of the vehicle. "We're overwhelmed, sir, but we'll get to her as soon as we can. Is there someone who can help her until we get there?"

Johnny raised his shoulders. "I guess I can. But I don't know that much."

"That's good enough."

Johnny watched the healthcare professionals rush to a man who was lying on the sidewalk, looking rather dead. He guessed the woman in his shop was not as bad as that poor fellow.

When he got back inside his store and kneeled next to the woman who was not rather dead, he tried Pacie's phone.

"Did the call go through?" the husband of the ill woman asked.

Johnny shook his head. "No, it didn't. But I told the paramedics that we needed help in here. They said they'd be here as soon as they can."

All Johnny could think of was Pacie. She could be dying somewhere and here he was, helping a stranger. But he would not leave. This woman needed his help, at least for the moment.

22

Shift

Shifting was the hard part indeed. Irma stalled the engine a few times before she managed to shift into the proper gear and get the sequence of the three pedals correct without coming to a jolting stop.

Finally the car moved out of Bart's reserved parking spot, through the lot, and toward the road. When Irma reached the road, she had to stop because of the bumper-to-bumper traffic. The car jerked and stalled when she hit the brake.

"Damn it." Irma slapped the steering wheel. "I forgot to press in the clutch."

Mr. Dibble looked at her as if to say, what are you doing?

"Don't worry, Mr. Dibble, I'll get it right. Eventually. I might end up owing Bart a new transmission before I'm done, but I've got to get to Pacie."

The slow-moving traffic on the road was tight. Horns honked as people were apparently trying to leave town. All

Irma wanted to do was get over to Pacie's house, a task that was looking like was going to take forever.

While Irma restarted the Mustang, a car stopped and waved for her to pull onto the road, and that's just what she tried to do. However, she was in such a nervous rush that she kept stalling the car. Soon the impatient man gave up on waiting for her to move and drove ahead, blocking her entrance until another car let her in.

"I wish Bart was here. I just hope he's not watching me destroy his car."

She got the car in gear and crept onto the road. Unfortunately, the traffic was stop-and-go, causing her driving to stall and sputter. This made the driver behind her blow his horn because she was not keeping up with the traffic, as slow as it was.

Irma considered pulling over and walking the rest of the way, but with hornets terrorizing the town, walking outside with no type of cover for protection was foolish. She would need to tough it out and continue the tortuous drive, and the people behind her would just have to suck it up.

Even if she were driving the Mustang like a pro, it was going to take a long time to reach the mansion. Hopefully, Pacie would be there when she arrived.

23

Downtown

Oscar could not believe what he was seeing as he drove through downtown toward the Harborside Jamboree. People were running around like crazed maniacs with arms flailing above screaming heads. The hornets themselves were easy to spot as their bird-sized bodies swooped at people and stung them. When the body fell to the ground—either from being rendered unconscious or simply from shock—they moved on to the next person.

With traffic at a standstill, people abandoned their vehicles and ran inside buildings. There was no way Oscar could drive any closer to the festival; he would need to leave his van where it sat on Main Street.

Oscar went in the back and donned his beekeeper suit. But based on what he was seeing, it would provide little, if any, protection.

He put on his backpack sprayer and left the van. He was outside the Good Old Days Antique Shop when he began spraying nearby flying hornets. Normally he would be spraying the nest, not random flying pests, but he had no idea where the nest was, but he would find it.

The stock pesticide he was using seemed to have no effect on the mutant insects, but it was possible the effect was delayed. He would use up the canister before switching to his special formula.

The entire downtown area was in utter confusion. He saw a teenager throw his cellphone, not necessarily aiming at Oscar, but it did whiz by his head, when the young man could not get it to work. Oscar dodged the small missile as he sprayed the hornets that now saw him as a prime target. It kept them away long enough for him to run back to his van to switch tanks.

He slammed the van door closed, attached his home-brewed concoction to the sprayer, said a quick prayer, and went back outside.

The hornets were smart; they were waiting for him to leave the van. Before they could sting him, he sprayed them, and they backed off. The formula appeared to be working better than the store-bought brand, but it was not knocking them out, nor stunning them. When he got back to his shop later, he would take a closer look at the captured hornet and come up with a better blend of pesticide.

Oscar battled the hornets for what seemed like an eternity but was less than an hour, as most people found shelter in the downtown stores.

He walked to the harbor where the festival had been and saw ambulances, police cars, and firetrucks blowing horns and sirens as they tried to get people to move their cars out of the way. A tow truck had to be used to clear abandoned vehicles off the road.

Having used up all his pesticides, Oscar walked back to his van. He saw a man looking out the antique shop's front window, waving him inside. He walked through the entrance to see what he wanted.

"Hey, man," Johnny said. "You can stay in here if you want. I'm Johnathon Armstrong, the store's owner."

The chaos that had been on the street was now within the shop, but at least there were no mutants flying around.

"Thanks. I'm Oscar of Oscar's Vermin Control. It looks like the hornets have left the area." Oscar removed his gloves and beekeeper's hood. "I used up all of my pesticide. I need to get back to my shop so that I can get more."

Johnny pointed out the window. "You're not going anywhere for a while. At least not until the traffic jam is cleared."

Oscar stared at the standstill. "Yep, I think you're right."

"I've got to get back to work," Johnny said. "We have injured people in here. Make yourself comfortable if you can."

"I won't be here long."

Oscar looked out the window again. Even if he drove on the sidewalk, which he couldn't, he would still not be able to leave downtown. He was here for as long as individuals remained sheltered within stores.

People sobbed inside the antique shop while others were curled atop blankets on the floor. Oscar watched Johnny tend to their needs as if he were a nurse or doctor rather than an antique dealer. He wondered if this was

Pacie's beau, because Irma had mentioned something that seemed very familiar to this place.

Oscar removed the backpack sprayer and the rest of his suit. He debated whether he should return them to the van now that the hornets were gone, or simply set the gear off to the side, just in case they came back.

He put the suit and sprayer on the floor next to a writing desk with pigeonholes and drawers, then stood at the window. His van was pinned in place until traffic moved out of the way, either in front or behind him. Right now, the only things in motion were people around an ambulance and faces through windows across the street.

Then he remembered Irma saying she lived above an antique store. This had to be the one because, as far as he knew, this was the only one in town.

Oscar walked up to Johnny, who was handing a handful of facial tissue to a sobbing woman.

"Johnathon," Oscar asked timidly. "Does Irma Foster live here?"

"Yeah, she lives one floor up, but I don't think she's home. If you want to check, just go through there," Johnny pointed toward the back of the shop, "and up the stairs. Her place is the only one on the second floor."

"Thanks for that," Oscar said. He half felt like he should be helping the shop owner tend to the crowd, but he wanted to ask Irma if she had a chance to see if she could read the faded address on the bee box.

Oscar walked to the back of the store through the door that Johnny had pointed to. He admired the old Otis scissor gate elevator for a moment before climbing the narrow staircase. When he got to the next floor, he knocked, but no one answered. He knocked again. He tried to open the door just in case Irma was collapsed on the floor from bee stings, but the door was locked.

"Irma, are you in there? It's Oscar." He supposed it was possible that she did not want to open the door for fear of a hornet flying inside. There was no answer.

Oscar walked back downstairs and saw Johnny kneeling by a woman who was having difficulty breathing. "Is there anything I can do to help?"

"Can you check on the ambulance and see when someone can help us? I asked them a while ago, and they said they'd come over here when they could." Johnny looked up at Oscar. "I don't want them to forget about us."

"I'll do that right now."

The woman's husband was angry. "They're taking too damned long."

"I think they're overwhelmed," Johnny said. "A lot of people need their help."

Oscar thought the husband was going to slug Johnny because he did not like his response.

"I'll be right back." Oscar placed a hand on Johnny's shoulder for a moment and then rushed to the front door. Seeing nothing flying around, he went outside and saw the ambulance preparing to leave.

Keys must have been left in ignitions because a couple of guys were moving cars to clear a path, even if it meant crashing into other vehicles and pushing them out of the way.

"Hey. Hey," Oscar shouted and waved as he ran up to the ambulance. "People in the antique shop need your help."

The driver rolled down his window. "We can't take any more people right now. We'll be back."

Oscar watched the ambulance scrape against vehicles, then ran back to the shop. The door's bell jingled violently as he burst through. He looked around for Johnny. Hopefully, the angry man had not punched Johnny and knocked him out.

"Oscar," Johnny said, walking up to him from another room. "What'd they say?"

"The ambulance is full, but they'll be back."

"My wife could be dead by then," the husband shouted from across the crowded room.

Oscar looked at the guy who was helping his wife sit up and drink from a bottle of water.

"It's all right, dear. They're doing the best they can," she said.

Oscar was relieved when he noticed the woman was now breathing easier and seemed fairly comfortable. "If you don't need my help, I'm going to put my gear in the van."

"I think everything is under control in here." Johnny lowered his voice. "That woman's husband is more work than his wife."

Oscar nodded. "Ain't that the truth?"

While Johnny walked back to the woman, Oscar gathered his suit and sprayer and went out to his van. He put the gear in the back and closed the door. He stood there, listening. Aside from horns blaring and angry shouts, it was eerily quiet on the street, as people stayed sheltered in the surrounding downtown shops.

Abandoned cars still trapped Oscar's van, but he figured if he needed to leave, he could move the cars that blocked his escape, like the men had done to the cars around the ambulance. Right now, the hornets were gone. If he could find the nest and the queen, he could stop them.

Oscar blinked hard a couple of times to remove any moisture from his eyes, then looked again at the blurry sky. It was now after six in the evening and a haze was settling on the city.

He removed his glasses, wiped the lenses on his shirt, and looked up again. "What's up with the sky? Is a storm a brewin'?"

Worried about Gary and Sadie, Oscar took his flip phone from his pocket. "Still no connection. I sure hope they're okay."

24

Biker

"I have to ditch this car." Gary looked in his rearview mirror. Cars were following behind him, but so far, no sirens and flashing lights were in pursuit.

Gary wiped his sweaty palms on the pant leg of his blue jeans. He could not believe what was happening. As far as he knew, his face was probably on the FBI's most wanted list. He needed to get to the college lab, but first, he would stop at Oscar's shop and figure something out.

The traffic was not moving fast enough. People not being allowed to leave town caused confusion. Finally, he reached Oscar's Vermin Control. He pulled behind the shop and parked his car so that it could not be seen from the road. Fortunately, there was an old green Gremlin from the nineteen-seventies parked there, too.

"I hope you run." Gary assumed Oscar must drive it because he saw the car's tire tracks in the gravel. "Oscar, you must be some genius mechanic to keep that ancient car running."

These days, Oscar probably used the ugly two-door hatchback when he drove to get groceries or such things.

Gary let Sadie out of the car and walked up to the jalopy, hoping it would start. Driving a car that the FBI— or whomever those people were—would not recognize would help him move incognito through town to the college with the specimen.

"Yes." It was unlocked, so he climbed into the driver's seat. No keys. He looked behind the visor, felt under the seat, and inside the glove compartment. They must be in the house.

Gary watched the cars on the road move along like a slow-moving caterpillar. He ran from behind the shop to the house. Sadie was right behind him.

Expecting the front door to be locked, he slowed to a stop. To his relief, it opened with a gentle turn of the knob. He and Sadie went inside. Sadie immediately went to her food and water dishes.

Gary stood there looking around. It surprised him that the interior of Oscar's house was clean and organized, something his workshop, or laboratory, was not. Aside from a coffee cup, there was not even a dirty dish in the kitchen sink.

"Keys, keys, I need keys." Gary looked on hooks, inside drawers, and wherever he thought the car keys could be, but he could not find them. Maybe Oscar had one set of keys and they were on a keychain hanging from his belt loop.

For a moment, he considered just hanging out in the house and forgetting about making his way to the college and examining the specimen that, based on his estimation, the government was after. Oscar's house looked airtight, and he and Sadie would be safe until this hornet catastrophe was over.

Although hanging out at Oscar's sounded like a good idea, he had to get the specimen to the lab. After all, a giant hornet with a camera on its back was bizarre, to say the least. It also meant there were dangerous thugs behind the scenes, especially when the residents of Black Water could not even leave town.

Gary sighed. "At this moment, I'm the only one who can figure this out. I have access to the college lab and the only specimen. I guess it's my duty, like it or not, to keep going. But how am I getting there?"

Hot and sweaty, mostly from nerves, Gary opened the refrigerator and took out a cold bottle of water. Taking a moment to nose around, he saw a partially eaten tater tot casserole, a block of some fancy cheese, and bottles of light beer. Then it occurred to him that maybe Oscar didn't live alone as he had assumed, and someone else could be in the house.

He quietly closed the refrigerator door. "Hello. Is anyone here?"

Sadie walked up to him. Gary patted her on the top of the head.

"Hello?"

No one else was there, at least on the first floor.

Gary put his empty water bottle in the trash can and looked out the kitchen window. Through the open doors of the backyard shed, Gary thought he saw a motorcycle. He walked outside with Sadie at his heels.

It was a small dirt bike. A 125cc, he estimated. Gary had not driven one since he was a teenager on the farm.

"Hallelujah." The keys were in the ignition.

Gary rolled the dirt bike into the yard. It had gas and appeared to be ready to ride. He sat on the worn seat. The bike's shocks had difficulty supporting Gary's weight as it sank toward the ground. He turned on the choke, pulled on the brake lever, and stomped on the kick starter. It took several tries, but Gary finally got it started.

A plume of exhaust fumes followed Gary as he drove it up to his car.

"This should fumigate the hornets." He laughed as he turned it off.

"You better start back up," Gary said, climbing off the bike.

He walked into the side door of the shop, looking for bungee straps or something that would secure the specimen lunchbox to the bike for the trip to the lab. The last thing he wanted was to lose the hornet on the way to the college.

"I can't believe I'm back here again," Gary said as he rummaged through shelves and drawers until he found various-sized straps. He untangled a couple that he thought would secure the lunchpail to the bike.

He walked out to the car. Leaving the toolbox, he took the lunchpail from the backseat, and strapped it down between the bike seat and the gas tank. The jury-rigged pail should hold until he got to the college.

He looked down at Sadie, who was inspecting his work. "You can't come with me. Let's get you inside the house. You'll be fine until Oscar gets back."

After putting Sadie in the house and refilling her water dish, he walked back outside. Saturday began crisp and clear, but now was muggy and hazy. The sun would set soon. He had better get going.

Gary groaned as he lifted a heavy leg over the bike's seat. He jiggled the specimen box, making sure it was secure for the trip and to see if the hornet was alive inside.

"Why'd you have to move when that agent had us pulled over?"

After a few kicks to the starter, the dirt bike spewed its toxic fumes. Gary coughed, then drove out from behind the shop and down the driveway to the nearly stopped bumper-to-bumper traffic.

"I guess I have to drive on the berm," he mumbled.

Gary drove down the gravel between the pavement and the ditch. As long as no one opened their passenger door into his path, he could get to the college in no time. The motorcycle was a blessing in disguise.

Every dip he hit caused his seat to rub against the tire. He felt bad that he was fumigating people who had their car windows down, but there was nothing he could do about it.

Gary buzzed along as he approached downtown. The sidewalk was empty when he drove onto it. He assumed that everyone had sought shelter inside buildings while they abandoned their cars in the street. He would make his way through town and then out to the college. At this rate, he would be there before dark.

Crossing the double-leafed drawbridge over Inky River was sketchy as he drove on the narrow path between the stopped cars and the railing. He cleared the bridge and turned onto the last road that would get him to the lab.

"Thank God I'm almost there."

Gary's smile turned to a scream when a semi-truck tractor turned in front of him, causing him to steer into a drain hole. The bike jackknifed, causing him to fly forward into a prickly bush. He looked at the truck and read Greg Gumby Trucking on the door.

"Hey," Gary yelled as he stood up and brushed himself off. He doubted the driver heard him because he kept trying to maneuver the truck-tractor on the shoulder of the road to get around the stopped vehicles in front of him.

Gary limped up to the truck that was stopped, unable to move any farther. He saw the driver look at him. "Hey, you just ran me off the road."

The driver ignored him.

Gary walked back to the dirt bike and lifted it upright. The front wheel was bent. "Damn it. Guess I gotta walk."

He removed the lunchpail and hobbled back to the semi. His leg was sore, but he managed to climb onto the passenger step. He banged on the window as the driver drove into the car ahead of him so that he could get around it. Gary banged on the window again.

The driver lowered the window. "Get off my truck."

"No." Gary surprised himself that he was not being his usual passive self. "You just made me wreck my bike. I need a ride to the college. It's just up the road."

"I'm not giving you a ride. Walk."

"My leg is sore."

"What's up with you people in this town?"

"I'm not leaving this step." Gary gripped the door handle with one hand and the specimen box with the other.

The driver rolled his eyes and rolled up the window as he kept pushing his truck ahead until he had cleared himself a path along the shoulder. The truck leaned to the side as it drove along the edge of the ditch. Gary felt as though the truck was going to tip over.

Gary banged on the window when they approached the college. "Stop. I'm here."

The driver shook his head, only slowing down. Gary would have to jump. He looked for a soft place to land. The lawn was his best bet. All he had to do was avoid hitting the Black Water College sign.

He leaped away from the truck. When he stopped rolling, he grabbed hold of his sore knee and yelled, "Asshole!"

The truck's air horn blasted a couple of deep notes as if saying, *have a good day*, as it drove away.

Gary at least felt a sense of satisfaction knowing that the trucker would be stopped at the armed roadblock that surely lay ahead.

Gary stood with a groan. He pulled down his mussed shirt and hobbled to the lunchpail that had rolled a good twenty feet away from the impact point. The lid had opened. He looked at the mutant hornet inside. It looked dead and battered.

"There's going to be nothing left of you by the time I get you to the lab."

Gary closed the lid and walked up to the college's main entrance, trying to ignore the excruciating pain in his knee and elbow. No one was at the college. Aside from a couple of cars, the parking lot was mostly empty. It was not totally surprising since it was a Saturday night. Even so, the campus had the same eerie feeling that was enveloping Black Water.

Past the glass doors, he saw no one inside the building. He pulled on the door, but it did not open. He tried another door, but that one would not open either. The college was locked up.

"Just my luck."

Gary brought his nose close to the glass; there was no one moving around inside. He looked back at the parking lot and saw a familiar car in staff parking. Hopefully, there was someone inside who could let him in. If it was security, they could be watching him with the cameras mounted throughout the campus.

But maybe whoever the car belonged to was not inside and had hitched a ride with someone else.

The college was a large building, and it had other entrances. After pounding on the glass and shouting for someone to let him in. He clutched the specimen under one arm and waved the other arm at a surveillance camera.

Gary shook his head. How was he getting inside? Was it possible a window was open? He doubted it. But a side door could be unlocked. That would more than likely be how whoever was inside, if anyone was inside, got into the building.

Gary looked at windows along the side of the building. He doubted any would be open because of the hornets. None were. However, some had a faint glow of light, as if lit by a weak safety light.

Then he noticed a security speaker on the wall next to the doors. Over the years, he had paid little attention to it, even though he had walked past it thousands of times.

Gary pressed the button next to the metal speaker box. Waited. Then pressed it again.

"Security, how may I help you?"

Relieved, Gary said, "I'm a student. I need to get inside."

"I'll be right there."

While he waited, he looked down the driveway toward the road. Vehicles were standing still. The road had become a parking lot itself. At least that asshole trucker was not in sight, but he was sure, if he kept watching the road, that the semi-truck would be heading back into town. If it was not, then good ol' Greg Gumby had tried to force his way through the blockade and was shot. Hopeful thinking.

The entrance door opened.

Gary turned and saw a young security guard. The yellow badge clipped to his chest pocket showed that his name was Kevin, and that he was a student. "Thanks, man. I need to get up to the entomology lab."

Kevin held the door open. "Hurry, get inside. There's something really odd going on around here."

Gary did not hesitate; he rushed inside.

"Thank you. I need to get up to the entomology lab," Gary said again.

"I've seen you before," Kevin said as he relocked the door. He turned toward Gary. "I'm a student, too, in electrical engineering. I do this gig to pick up some extra money."

"I've seen you around, too." Gary held out a sweaty palm for a handshake. "I'm Gary."

They shook hands, then headed to the elevator.

"You must be hungry." Kevin nodded toward the lunchpail.

At first, Gary was not sure what Kevin was talking about. "Oh, well, not really."

They walked inside the elevator.

"Can you believe what's happening?" Kevin pressed the button to the second floor. "We're safe inside the college, at least as far as I can tell. I decided I'm better off staying on duty until this thing blows over."

"Hopefully, they pay you all the overtime you deserve."

They laughed.

The elevator door opened Kevin followed Gary out and down to the entomology lab and inside.

Gary did not want someone seeing the deformed hornet and possibly reporting it. He sat the lunchpail on a table.

"I have it from here," Gary said.

"Okay. I'll be doing rounds or in the security office if you need me."

Kevin was walking out the lab door when Gary said, "Do you know anything about radio transmitters and things like that?"

"Yeah, I know a bit about it. Why do you ask?"

"The work I'm doing involves some of that. Do you mind if I contact you later if I have questions about that stuff?"

"Not at all. I've been rather bored and would love to help you. You'll need to use the lab phone and call the security office. For some reason, cellphones aren't working. It's as though the signal is being blocked rather than cell towers being down."

That made sense to Gary. "I'm sure I'll be calling you later. I just need to get my . . . experiment set up first."

"Cool beans."

Gary watched Kevin leave the lab. He knew he would call him for help. But first, he needed to remove the device strapped to the hornet.

PART IV
Dark Knight

25

Listen

Pacie grew impatient. She could not stay in the dank wine cellar any longer. It was quiet on the other side of the door. The hornets seemed to have given up on trying to get to her. Maybe they were busy doing what they were doing when she first went down into the basement, likely building a nest.

She said a prayer, put her phone in the back pocket of her blue jeans, and ever so slowly began pulling away everything she had stuffed into the cracks of the door. If the hornets were waiting on the other side, they would certainly stir, and she would hear them. But so far, all she heard was a distant low droning sound.

As quietly as she could, she kept removing plastic and dirt until enough had been removed so that she could open the door.

With her hands on the door handle and a foot at the bottom of the door for counter pressure, she gently and slowly pulled. Not as slow as Edgar A. Poe's, The Tell-Tale Heart:

> *I moved it slowly—very, very slowly, so that I might not disturb the old man's sleep. It took me an hour to place my whole head within the opening so far that I could see the old man as he lay upon his bed.*

No, Pacie was not as patient as that poor fellow.

She was ready to push it back closed, but so far, it was unnecessary. The door creaked, but any hornets that were out there did not seem to notice or had left the basement. Hopefully, the latter.

When Pacie had the door open enough so that she could squeeze through, she did. She looked at the end of the hallway from where the hornets had come from earlier. The hornets were still there, busy working on what appeared to be a gigantic nest.

She froze in place as her mind tried to process what they were building. It was not natural for an insect to build something so large that it filled the whole exit. But this . . . this was supernatural.

There was no time to make sense of what she saw, nor to take a picture. She had to get out of there. Creep or run was the question. She would tiptoe as quietly as she could to the stairs leading to the main floor.

As she moved ever so slowly, she decided she would take a picture after all, to document what the mutants were intelligently creating. She was sure her phone was set to not make a clicking sound when a picture was taken.

Pacie held the phone up and snapped a shot at the hornets and their creation. It clicked. The sound caught the hornets' attention. There was a moment, a split second, where they seemed to stare at each other. Then the hornets shot toward her. Pacie dropped the phone and ran up the stairs, closing the door behind her just in time.

She locked it and backed away, ready to run to the next room with a door, but it was unnecessary. The hornets were unable, or unwilling, to get through.

Pacie ran into the study, slamming the door shut behind her, along with every door leading into the room. She was shaking as she stood still, listening. The hornets must have gone back to working on their project.

She reached into her pocket to retrieve her phone, then remembered she had dropped it in the basement. Fortunately, the desk had a landline phone.

First, she called Irma, but the call did not go through, along with her calls to her daughter, granddaughter, and Johnny's cellphone.

Pacie thought for a moment. Bart would know how Irma was doing. She found the business card he handed them and called the marina phone; Tara answered.

"May I speak to Bart, please?"

"He's kinda busy right now." Tara's voice quivered. "May I take a message?"

"This is Pacie Rose. I was wondering how Irma was doing; she was with him today."

"Oh, yeah. She was fine earlier, but she's not here now."

"Where'd she go?"

"I don't know. It's been such a chaotic mess here that I hardly know what's going on."

"If you hear from Irma, can you have her call me?"

"Sure, I can do that."

Pacie hung up the phone. Irma could be holing up in a room some place at the marina since she was not right there in the marina's lobby.

"Maybe you know something, Oscar." Pacie took the phone book from the bottom of her desk drawer and found the phone number to Oscar's Vermin Control and dialed it. After it rang a few times, an answering machine picked up. Pacie left a message for him to call her.

Then she found the phone number for the college. After listening to a robot have her push button after button, she finally reached the entomology lab.

"Gary."

"Gary, it's Pacie. I'm so happy that I got through to you. I haven't had good luck reaching people on the phone.

"Pacie, glad you called. Only landline-to-landline calls go through. Apparently, cellphones are being blocked."

"That explains it. What are you doing? I hope you've been able to check that freakish hornet that was caught in my wasp trap."

"As a matter of fact, I'm about to do that right now. I don't want to say much over the phone, but are you able to come over here?"

"I'll drive there when I hang up."

"Don't bother driving. I don't know if you've looked out at the road, but traffic isn't moving. It's gridlocked."

"Oh, wow. I can't see the road from my house. Actually, hornets have had me trapped in my basement. I finally escaped. It's rather dangerous around my house right now."

"If you don't live too far away, you could ride a bike or walk if you had to."

"I don't live too far away from the college. It's just on the other side of the woods," Pacie said. "I'll get out there one way or the other."

"If you run into FBI agents, or whoever they are, don't entirely trust them."

"Really?"

"Really. There's something going on and it's not good. The whole town is quarantined and no one can leave. That's why the traffic is jammed. I think it has something to do with the hornets."

"Are you there alone?"

"I'm alone in the lab, but Kevin, the security guy, is in the building. When you reach the main entrance, push the security button and he'll let you in. I'll let him know you're on the way."

"Be careful, Gary."

"I will. See you soon."

Pacie was shaking when she hung up the phone. She looked inside her satchel and made sure the EpiPen was there. She slung it over her shoulder and stood still, not only listening for the buzzing of bees but whether to take Gary's word that the roads were impassable.

She picked up her car keys and quietly walked outside. There was loud humming on the side of the house by the exterior basement entry.

She knew that starting the SUV could get their attention, yet it was a safer place to be, rather than out in the open if she walked down the driveway to see if there were actually cars packed on the road.

As quietly as she could, she opened the car door, and once inside, pulled it only closed enough to stop any dinging sounds. She turned the key, waiting for the vehicle to be swarmed. It was not.

She drove slowly down the long driveway, only to stop when she saw that what Gary said was true. There was no way she was going to reach the college any time soon.

She backed up and drove up to the garage where her bicycle was inside.

Moving around the property unsheltered was scary. If the hornets noticed her, one EpiPen would not save her.

She went into the garage, closing the side entrance door behind her. She walked over to her bike and rolled it toward the door. That's when she noticed it had a flat tire.

"Great. By the time I'm able to fix this, I could've driven there." Pacie put the kickstand back down. "Guess I gotta walk."

Pacie went out of the garage and looked toward the forest. She would take the overgrown path to the college. There would be only one road to cross.

Pacie felt like running, but instead strode across the lawn, through the old fruit trees, and past the long empty oxen paddock to the woods and walked down the path.

Her heart would thump when she stepped on a branch and it cracked. All she could envision was the hornets racing toward her like an arrow, but it did not happen. They seemed to be preoccupied with the hive.

An hour of stumbling through the dark woods had passed when she approached the road. She cringed when she heard the occasional car horn beep. The sound would easily attract the hornets.

The college driveway was on the other side of the road. She walked between the cars with angry drivers, then up the driveway to the main entrance. She saw the callbox that Gary had mentioned and pushed the button. Then she tried to open the locked doors.

A moment later, a voice said, "May I help you?"

"Hi, I'm Pacie Rose. I need to get to the lab where Gary is."

"Oh, yeah, he told me. I'll be right there."

While she waited, she heard what sounded like a gunshot in the distance. And then another.

Kevin opened the door and Pacie rushed inside.

"I thought I heard a gunshot," Pacie said, watching Kevin relock the door.

"It probably was. There are a lot of bad things going on." Kevin walked to the stairs. "I'll take you to Gary."

"Thank you."

"I don't trust the elevators anymore. I've got the feeling they're going to cut the power next."

"They?"

Their footsteps echoed in the concrete stairwell.

"Yeah, whoever is keeping us trapped in town and blocking signals. It's like they're going to nuke us next."

At that moment, Pacie realized just how serious this whole situation was. It was not just about finding the queen and eliminating the hornets; it was a matter of life and death beyond the bees.

"This can't be kept secret. The country must know what's going on here," Pacie said.

"Maybe," Kevin opened the second-floor door. "But no one from town can reach anyone outside the city limits. And from what I saw on the news before it went to static, was that a deadly virus had overtaken Black Water and that's why no one can come or go. I know this will sound crazy, but it's as though the government is going to kill everyone in Black Water just to get rid of those wasps."

Pacie walked down the hallway next to Kevin. "Or hide their existence."

Kevin opened the door to the lab. "I brought you, Ms. Pacie Rose."

Gary looked up from a dissection tray. "Pacie, you won't believe what I've found."

Kevin followed her to Gary.

"What do you have?" Pacie said, standing next to the table.

"Here, take a look." Gary sat down the scalpel he was using and opened the metal lunchpail from Oscar's. With his gloves still on, he removed the device and held it in his hand for Pacie to see.

A piece of metal the size of a mint candy lay in his palm. "What am I looking at?"

"It's just as I suspected when I saw it at Oscar's, a camera with some kind of receiver, transmitter attached."

"Is it working?"

"I don't know, but I think it is. I've been keeping it in that metal lunchpail to stop some of that."

"I want to see it," Kevin said, moving in close. After a moment, he wrote on the notepad next to a microscope, BE QUIET! He held it up for them to see.

Then Kevin wrapped the camera apparatus in a paper towel and put it back into the lunchbox. Then wrote, WE SHOULD HIDE THIS.

Gary took the pad and wrote, I WAS WORRIED ABOUT THAT.

Kevin wrote, THEY MIGHT RAID THE LAB OR KILL US.

"What?" Gary said aloud, his eyes wide.

"It's nothing. You can probably just throw it away." Pacie said, then wrote, LET'S LEAVE IT IN THE LUNCHROOM INSIDE THE FRIDGE SO THEY CAN'T TRACK IT HERE.

Kevin nodded.

Pacie said aloud, "Let's get out of here."

Kevin wrote, BEFORE WE HIDE IT, MAYBE I CAN TAP INTO ITS SIGNAL.

Gary ripped off the scribbled page, crumpled it up, and wrote on the one below, HOW?

Kevin took his cellphone from his pocket and opened an app. He held it next to the device and adjusted settings on the phone.

Pacie and Gary both gave him a confused look.

Then, from the phone's speaker, the sound of someone speaking could be heard through the static.

"Is the drop still on for three?"

"It is. Unfortunately, we have no choice if we want to keep knowledge of Dark Knight from getting out."

"The parameter barriers are almost all in place. We'll pull the agents and troops out soon."

The three in the lab could not believe what they were hearing.

Pacie wrote on the notepad, DOES ANYONE KNOW WHAT THEY'RE TALKING ABOUT?

Gary and Kevin shook their heads.

Kevin wrote, IT MUST BE COMING FROM SOMEPLACE CLOSE BY.

Then they heard through the speaker, "Someone's listening in."

"Who?"

"I don't know. It might be coming from inside the college."

"Find who it is and silence them."

26

Hum

After accidentally turning on the wipers and pulling out the cigarette lighter, Irma finally figured out how to turn on the Mustang's headlights. At last the traffic moved, but when she approached the next intersection, a tall razor-wire fence sat behind concrete blocks. There was no way anyone could go any farther. It forced vehicles to either turn left or right and travel roads along the perimeter of the town.

Irma did not want to leave Black Water, at least not yet. She just wanted to get to Pacie's house and make sure she was okay.

As she followed a zigzag path to Pacie's, she tried to reach her by phone for the hundredth time, but there was not even a signal.

Irma looked over at Mr. Dibble, who was sitting up in the passenger seat watching the road ahead. "I'm about to pull my hair out, but I don't want to do that because it's already too thin."

Mr. Dibble looked over at Irma as she lit a cigarette. "It's taking me ten times longer than normal just to get to Pacie's."

Feeling a little more comfortable with her driving skills, she pulled into Pacie's driveway and drove down it until she saw the SUV in the driveway.

"She's home." Relieved, Irma pulled up behind Pacie's vehicle.

There were no lights on inside the mansion. Irma knocked on the door. "Maybe she's not home."

Irma opened the door and walked inside.

"Pacie, are you here?" Irma said loudly as she closed the door.

All she heard was the grandfather clock ticking in the foyer.

"Pacie, it's Irma." She turned on the foyer light and then walked through the green dining room to the study. Hopefully, everything was all right.

She walked up to the desk and noticed the phone book, and papers scattered on the top. "Who were you trying to call? Did someone pick you up?"

On the likely chance that Pacie could be lying unconscious from anaphylactic shock somewhere in the house, Irma first searched the downstairs rooms before moving up to the second and third floors. All that was left to search was the garage and basement. When she got back downstairs, she walked through the laundry room to a door that led into the garage. She turned on the light.

"Pacie, are you out here?"

Then she noticed the bike with a flat tire. "I think she was trying to leave, Mr. Dibble. Let's find a flashlight and look around outside."

Irma looked on the shelves in the garage until she found a flashlight hanging from a hook above the workbench. She tapped it on her hand a few times to stop it from flickering and walked through the garage and out into the foggy chill of the night.

With Mr. Dibble at her side, she walked around the side of the garage to the lakeside of the mansion. Irma continued to shout out Pacie's name as she walked onto the piazza.

Although Pacie lived outside the outskirts of town, the surrounding sounds seemed muffled. She heard a helicopter flying nearby but could not see the lights. No starlight penetrated through the mist and the lake was quiet. Aside from a low hum, Irma felt as though she was enveloped with a damper system. It was either that or her ears were plugged.

When Irma stepped off the piazza and turned the corner to the south side of the house, Mr. Dibble began growling. The humming sound now buzzed. She shined the flashlight on the sloped wall cellar door, stopping in her tracks. As she tried to make sense of what she saw bulging around the double doors, a sharp tingle of nerves rushed through her body. It seemed like an eternity had passed before she realized what she was looking at, but it had to be only a few seconds.

A beehive. A huge nest ballooned out around the cellar door and likely oozed inside the basement.

Mr. Dibble began barking. That was all it took for the mutant hornets to spot her. They flew toward her. Irma ran back around to the piazza and to the door.

"Please don't be locked." Irma's voice squeaked as she tried to push air through tense vocal cords.

Irma opened it and she and Mr. Dibble shot inside. She slammed it closed and turned the lock as the hornets thrust their bodies against the door's wooden panels like giant hail pellets.

She backed away from the door while Mr. Dibble kept barking.

Fearing the hornets would break through a window, she ran into the study, making sure all the doors were closed. This had to be the safest place, at least for now.

Irma quieted Mr. Dibble. She did not want the hornets to follow the barking. She listened for shattering glass and buzzing, but heard none. They must have given up. Their nest must be more important than pursuing an old woman and her dog.

She kneeled on the floor, hugging Mr. Dibble. "Now what? This must be what happened to Pacie, but where could she have gone?"

Feeling protected, at least for the moment, Irma sat at the desk. She looked at her cellphone and saw there still was no signal. She picked up the landline phone and dialed Pacie's cell, but it did not work. Irma called Amanda and Charlotte and got the same result. Even Oscar's cellphone would not receive a call.

"Maybe the problem is with the cellphones; I'll try Oscar's shop."

Irma thumbed through the open phone book and dialed the shop. The call went through.

"Oscar's Vermin Control." Oscar sounded out of breath.

"Thank goodness, I can't believe I got a hold of you."

"I just walked in the shop. Is this Irma?"

"It is. Have you seen Pacie? She's not home and I can't reach her by phone. I'm worried she might be in trouble."

"No, I haven't. I saw Johnny and a bunch of sick people," Oscar said, his breath eased. "I was trapped downtown for a while until traffic finally started movin'. It took forever and a day to get back here."

"I know what you mean; I had the same problem." Irma paused. "But I think I found what has to be the super nest."

"No shit? Where?"

"It's at Pacie's house. They're building it around the basement door, on the south side of the building. Are you able to get over here? I think I'm pretty much trapped in the study right now."

"Stay there and don't go anywhere. Before I leave, I need to see if Gary left a message and check if Sadie's safe."

"Be careful because those hornets chased me and Mr. Dibble into the house. I'd hate to think what would've happened if the swarm had caught us."

"I'm going to make a slight modification to my pesticide, and then I'll be right over."

Irma hung up the phone and noticed the pieces of paper from the mail package setting off to the side of the desk. "I'll work on these."

While Mr. Dibble laid down on a fluffy rug next to a wing chair, Irma woke up Pacie's computer. Knowing her cousin used the same four digits for most of her personal identification numbers, she was able to login and download the software she needed to decipher the faded addresses.

She signed in to her account and scanned the labels to a higher quality than what Pacie had emailed her. With a little puzzle solving, she would be able to read the text and determine who the bees were being sent to, and where they came from.

27

Hide

Gary tossed his gloves on the floor, picked up the lunchpail holding the device, and followed Kevin and Pacie out of the entomology lab, limping from his sore knee.

The panel above the elevator showed the car rising from the basement as they ran past it to the stairwell. Gary gently closed the door behind them as the elevator dinged.

They ran so fast down the stairs that Pacie felt as though she were flying. They reached the first floor and ran down the hallway to the cafeteria, with Gary lagging behind.

"This way." Kevin led them into the kitchen to the refrigerators in the back.

Gary chose the closest one and slid the lunchbox to the back of a shelf, then placed large bags of frozen corn in front of it. "Now what?"

"We need to stop them," Pacie said, out of breath.

"How? And from doing exactly what?" Gary asked.

Pacie looked at Kevin. "Where in the college do you think they are?"

"The basement?" Kevin shrugged.

"You're the security guard around here. Shouldn't you know everyone who's in the building?" Gary asked.

"I'm a student guard, so there are some places off limits to me."

"Is there a lab in the basement?" Pacie pushed her hair away from her forehead.

Kevin shrugged again. "I don't know. The security office is in the basement, but most of the rest of that level is off limits to me."

"That's probably where they're at," Pacie said.

"Oh shit," Gary said. "I left the Vespa Anna I was dissecting on the table. If they go in there, they'll see it and know that we know what they're up to."

"They'll for sure be after us," Pacie said, listening for sounds of people running.

"That's what they said on the app," Kevin said, holding his phone. "And what's a Vespa Anna?"

"That's just what I'm calling it; a cross between an Asian giant hornet and an Anna's hummingbird. The ultimate killing machine for the military. Max thinks it's a clandestine operation."

Kevin nodded. "That explains why they want to trap everyone, except for themselves, in Black Water and then drop something on us. To kill us so that we can't talk."

"It's crazy," Pacie said, "but it makes the most sense."

"But how are we going to stop them?" Gary asked. "I doubt any of us have had training in how to do that kind of thing."

"Dumb luck." Kevin laughed.

Pacie shushed him. "Quiet. I think they're coming."

They fumbled around like clowns in a circus until Kevin opened a closet door and the three of them squeezed inside.

Pacie winced. "Someone's stepping on my foot."

"Sorry," Kevin said as he moved his foot and pushed a broom to the side. "There's no room and I can't see."

"Quiet." Gary pressed his body against the wall.

Kevin opened the security application on his phone, revealing streaming video from the college's cameras. He pulled up the one to the hallway in front of the cafeteria. It showed two men dressed in black suits, carrying some type of long gun, making their way down the hallway, examining rooms along the way.

"They look like the mob," Gary said as he rested a foot on the rim of a mop bucket.

"Or men in black," Kevin said.

"Is there a back door?" Pacie asked as she pushed Gary's arm away from her waist. "Maybe we can make a run for it."

"There is, but it's too far away." Kevin kept watching the video. "They'll be in the cafeteria before we can escape."

"They're talking," Pacie said, pulling her satchel to the front to give Gary and Kevin more room. "Can you turn it up a little? For only a minute."

"This whole operation is a joke," the man holding a tracking device said. "Whose bright idea was it to send the secret weapon by mail rather than private currier, anyway?"

"Who knows?" the other said as he tried to open a locked door. "All I know is that we have to find the device and the person who took it."

"Don't bother with that door," the man said, looking at the handheld screen. "It's in the cafeteria, for sure. Whoever took it is probably in there, too."

The two men rushed into the cafeteria, their guns at the ready. The man with the tracking device followed the signal back to the refrigerator where Gary had placed the lunchpail.

Kevin turned off the volume on his phone and the three of them watched the men remove the lunchbox from the shelf. "So much for metal blocking the signal."

One of the men opened it. "It's here." He placed it into a pouch attached to his belt.

The other man used his walkie-talkie to contact someone. "We found the device. What do you want us to do?"

"Find whoever took it and bring them to me. He can't be far away."

Pacie could not breathe as she watched the men get closer. They tossed stainless steel pans around and pulled items out of cupboards large enough to house a body, making lots of noise and an enormous mess along the way.

Was it possible they would overlook the broom closet?

No. The door was yanked opened and the three of them stood motionless in the semi-light as if they were brooms and mops to be ignored. But they weren't.

With guns aimed directly at them, they raised their arms in surrender and said nothing.

"Step out," the short man shouted.

The other man pulled out his walkie-talkie. "We have him and two others."

"Bring them to me," a gruff voice said.

28

Chili

Irma slowly read the addresses as she interpreted them. "Let's see. It came from the DoD. What is that? The Department of Defense? It is from Washington, DC. And was headed to Black Water College."

Irma jumped when she heard a car door close. She looked at the desk clock; it was after eleven.

"That must be Oscar."

Instead of leaving the study and going to the door, she stayed in the bee free room, hoping Oscar would just walk inside the mansion.

There was a knock and Mr. Dibble barked.

"Irma, it's Oscar."

Irma opened the study door and shouted through the dining room. "Come in. I'm in the study."

Oscar was dressed in his beekeeper's suit with the sprayer slung on his back, carrying a cage, as he followed Irma's voice into the dining room. He walked with a stiff gait as he approached Irma. "Are you all right?"

"In here." Irma motioned for him to come into the study. "Are there any bees inside?"

"I didn't see any, but I haven't really looked around yet."

"Why are you walking like that? I didn't realize bee suits were that cumbersome."

"They're not." Oscar sat down the cage he was carrying and took off his headlamp, then removed his hood and gloves, setting them on the table next to the computer. "I've just wrapped myself in Kevlar fabric for extra protection. Have you seen the stingers on those things?"

"They're long, for sure," Irma said, watching a bead of perspiration roll down Oscar's face. "Bulletproof vests are made of Kevlar, aren't they? How'd you happen to have any of that?"

"I bought it a while back so that I could make myself protective sleeves and gloves. I deal with rodents, and they have sharp teeth."

"That's smart thinking."

Oscar looked at the computer screen. "Is that the bee packaging label?"

"It is. I just deciphered it." Irma sat at the desk. "As best as I can tell, it has the return address as the Department of Defense and its destination was Black Water College, room . . . 0116, I believe. Or it could be 0115."

"I'm not surprised because those things flyin' around are the shadow government's secret weapon." He wiped his moist forehead with the back of his hand. "Have you heard from Pacie or anyone yet?"

"I haven't heard from anyone. How about you?"

"Gary left a message. He said that he was heading over to the college. I called the number he wrote down, but no one answered. And I saw Johnny, like I said, but Pacie wasn't there."

"Who's Gary?"

"He's a graduate student at the college. He was helping me with the hornet problem."

Irma looked down at Mr. Dibble, who was sniffing the legs of Oscar's beekeeper suit. "Is Sadie all right?"

"She's safe and sound in the house."

"That's good to hear." Irma sighed. "So, all we have to do is get rid of that nest, find Pacie, and make sure everyone is healthy."

"We'll need to catch the queen." Oscar turned toward the door. "Well, I need to get to work. You and Mr. Dibble stay here. I'll come back inside when I'm done."

"Okay, and be careful because I doubt I'll have much luck getting you to the hospital."

"Do you know where the basement door is? I'll take a look at the hive from the inside of the house first."

"It's under the central staircase."

"Don't open the basement door. I want to keep those critters out of the main body of the house."

Oscar donned his gear and left to hopefully put an end to the hornet mess.

Irma looked at Mr. Dibble. "Let's watch him from the grand room. He did say he didn't see any hornets in the house."

She walked through the dining room and central passage past the staircase. Then through the front parlor and into the grand room with its tall, arched palladium windows. Putting her nose to the glass, she could see the nest encasing the cellar door below her.

"The hornets are getting riled up. Oscar must be spraying in the basement."

Moments later, Irma heard the basement door open and close with a bang. She rushed to the parlor and saw Oscar running.

"Oscar, is everything okay?"

He did not answer as he rushed outside with a hornet right behind him. Irma slammed the parlor door shut and ran back into the grand room, where she made sure all the doors and windows were securely closed. She did not know if the hornet that was chasing Oscar had followed him through the exterior door or was inside the house.

Through the glass, Irma watched as Oscar came around the corner of the mansion and stopped. She could tell he was surprised by what he was looking at.

He cautiously walked toward the hive and began spraying the horde of hornets as they swarmed him. Fortunately, the formula he was using made them drop to the ground. Irma watched as he put them into the metal cage that looked like a large cat carrier.

Irma smiled and swung a fist into the air. "You go, Oscar."

Her heart pounded, fearing for Oscar's life as he shot sprays of pesticide, or whatever he was using, at the mutants. When there were no more hornets to spray, he collected them off the ground and caged them before he began tearing apart the nest.

"I think he did it, Mr. Dibble."

Irma gasped when a hornet, larger than the others, emerged from the hive. It stung Oscar in the chest and then flew away. Oscar clenched the front of his suit and fell backward.

Irma shook and brought a hand to her sternum as if she was the one that had gotten stung. She banged on the window, hoping he would hear her. "I think he's dead, Mr. Dibble."

Moments later, Oscar struggled to stand like an ancient Egyptian mummy and looked at the window. He waved at Irma, picked up the cage, and walked back to his work van.

Irma waved back, surprised he was alive. She looked down at the shredded nest. "Is he done?"

It was not long before Oscar came back inside. Irma met him in the central passage.

"I thought you were dead."

Oscar removed his hood and pulled the Kevlar strips of fabric from his head that were wrapped like a scarf and dropped them on an entryway bench. "Me, too. I'm surprised the aramid fibers worked so well."

"Does this mean you got them all?"

"All except the queen. She took off after she tried to sting me."

Irma rubbed her forehead. "I'm getting a headache."

"Me too." Oscar took off the rest of his suit and Kevlar, then unbuttoned his sleeveless flannel shirt and looked at his chest. "Did the queen bee leave a mark?"

Irma looked at his bony ribcage. "I don't see anything except a red spot."

Oscar re-buttoned his shirt. "I'll probably have a bruise tomorrow because I felt it jab at me like it had a filet knife attached to its freakin' hairy body."

"So what happens now?"

"I'm gonna bag up the hive and take it back to my shop. I'll let Gary take some of it for his studies. But I don't know what I'm going to do with the hornets, yet. Other than make sure they don't escape when they wake up—if possible."

"You'd better because I can't go through much more of this." Irma shivered. "What did you have in your sprayer? It certainly did the job."

Oscar smiled as though he had just won an InkyFest sweepstakes prize for a year's worth of free cheeseburgers from Captain Burger. "I revised my formula and I'm happy to say it worked like expected."

"Except that it killed those hornets. I know they were deadly, but I still hated to see them die."

"Oh, they're not dead. They're only stunned. They'll come out of it later, so I'll need to get them back to the shop and double cage them."

"How are you going to catch the queen?"

"I'm not sure yet. But I'll figure it out."

Irma's eyes widened and her jaw dropped as she looked at Oscar.

"What's wrong? You're lookin' at me as though I grew another head."

"Uh, look in the mirror." Irma pointed to a mirror over the entryway console table.

Oscar walked up to the mirror and gulped when he saw his reflection. "My face is red as Cap'n Burger's hot chili. Must be the capsaicin I added to my formula."

"I thought it was smelling like taco Tuesday around here." Irma laughed. "You must be having a bad reaction to it. Can you breathe all right?"

"So far." Oscar began scratching his cheeks. "It itches like hell."

Irma could not stop laughing.

"What's so funny? Do you like to see a man in misery?"

"I'm sorry, but it's the funniest thing I've seen in a while."

Oscar's nails scraped his skin, leaving wretched lines. "I'm glad I could put some joy in this otherwise dreadful night. I should charge you extra for the pleasure." Oscar frowned. "Do you have any itching cream?"

Irma put a hand over her mouth, trying to hold back a belly laugh. "I'm sure Pacie has something. Follow me to the bathroom."

29

Stinger

Pacie stumbled over a dustpan as she exited the broom closet with her hands up.

"You're not going to get away with this," Kevin said. "I'm security here and I'm reporting you."

The two men in black sneered as they kept their guns pointed at the trio.

"Move it," the tall man said.

Pacie did not know where to move it to, so she kept walking to the cafeteria door of which they had come in. She opened the door and walked into the cold hallway.

"Keep going," the man said in a nasty tone. "Take the stairwell to the basement."

Gary limped next to Pacie as they made their way down the steps, exiting on the basement level. They made brief eye contact and Pacie could tell he wanted to say something but did not dare.

"Hang a left at the end of the hall," one of the men said.

The possibilities of what was going to happen to them flashed through Pacie's mind as they turned into the next hallway. Were they going to be questioned? Released? Imprisoned? Or tortured and murdered? They would find out soon enough.

"Stop." One of the men moved around them and walked up to the door of an unassigned lab room, labeled only 0115. He punched in a keypad code and stepped inside. "Get in here. Now!"

The three of them went into the room, not that they had a choice. A big linebacker-type man stood near what looked like radio equipment. He closed a black suitcase and looked up at them.

"What do you want us to do with them, Cap?" one of the gun toting men asked. "They know too much."

What worried Pacie was that they were letting them see their faces. One thing Pacie knew—from watching movies—was that if the bad guys let you see their face, you would soon be six feet under.

The big man grunted. Then with a baritone voice said, "Tie 'em up."

One of the men retrieved a roll of gray duct tape from a shelf and tied Pacie and the others' hands behind their back. He then forced them to set on the hard tile floor.

"They can recognize us," the other man said.

"It won't matter," Cap said. "I'll move the drop up to one and have them increase the potency."

"Strong enough to kill 'em?"

"Of course. By the time anyone ventures into town, everyone will be dead from the virus."

"What virus?" Pacie asked.

"The virus that's quarantining this town. It's deadly and extremely contagious."

"You're just covering up for the murderous hornets," Gary said. "What are they, some illegal weapon of war?"

"To be precise," Cap said, "an unapproved weapon of war. It was developed to aid marines and soldiers on the battlefield, to save lives, not destroy. The intentions were good."

"Why was it not approved?" Pacie asked.

Cap watched the two men in black, pack some of the electronic equipment carefully into a trunk. "They said it was too unpredictable because of the animal nature of it, but I told them they were wrong. We had them trained to follow instructions from the transceiver attached and embedded in their bodies, but they unfortunately were allowed to escape."

"Yeah," one man piped up. "Your incompetent postal service is to blame. This is the most inept town I've been in, and I'll be glad to leave."

Pacie kept twisting her wrists, trying to break through the strong tape. "But why not just catch it and have that be the end of it? Why are you killing everyone in town?"

Cap laughed. "Isn't it obvious? It's a secret weapon and the enemy can't know what we're doing. If they knew, they would build counter-weapons to the stingers and we will have lost the element of surprise. That's why everyone in your wretched town has contracted a deadly virus and cannot leave its boundary under any circumstance."

Pacie shook her head. "So that's why you put a total blackout on the town. But what you're doing is murder. You're killing innocent people."

"Cap," one man called out. "The stingers are still at the mansion, but the queen has left. Something's happened."

Pacie jerked at the mention of a mansion. Black Water had more than one mansion. "Mansion? Which mansion?"

No one answered.

"Seven, you stay here and finish packing equipment," Cap said, picking up the suitcase. "Eleven, you and I will head over to the hive."

As Cap and Eleven prepared to leave, another man in black burst through the door, struggling with a male citizen whose hands were secured behind his back. Pacie recognized him as the trucker with a bad attitude that she had been encountering.

"Greg Gumby," Pacie mumbled as she read the words Greg Gumby Trucking on his T-shirt. She did not say his name as a greeting, but as a statement of irritation.

"Who's that?" Cap asked, annoyed.

"A damned troublemaker," the man said, pushing him onto the floor next to Pacie and the others.

"Why'd you bring him here?"

The man looked at Cap as he taped Greg's ankles together. "You know. To dispose of him."

"In less than an hour they'll be gone," Cap said, opening the lab door.

"Wait," Pacie shouted. "It's not going to be so easy to kill us. People are going to know that a chemical or whatever has been dropped on us and you'll be arrested for murder."

"Mass murder," Kevin added.

Cap smiled. "No one is going to see us spread the poison and if they do, it's an antidote to save the citizens from the killer virus, not harm them."

"But they'll know the chemical killed us," Pacie said. "The autopsies will prove it."

"The chemical mimics the virus. All deaths will be attributed to the virus, that's why the town is quarantined. No one can enter it until you plebs are dead. The authorities know that if they come in here before the virus has burned itself out, they risk infecting the rest of the country, or world for that matter." Cap walked out the door, laughing.

"Virus?" Greg said as he fought the restraints.

"We'll explain later," Gary said.

"By the sounds," Greg said, "there isn't going to be a later."

Eleven finished packing the equipment and rolled the trunk into the hallway. But before he closed the door, he sat a black metal box on the floor. He punched a few buttons and the ticking of a clock sounded.

"You kids have fun with the stinger. I gave you a few extra minutes to think about your fate," Eleven said as he closed the door. He could be heard laughing as the trunk rumbled down the hallway.

30

Secret

With anti-itch cream spread all over Oscar's face, Irma went to the kitchen to get the large garbage bags he wanted.

"You can keep the roll," Irma said, handing the box to Oscar.

"Are you expecting someone?" Oscar asked. "I heard a car door."

Irma grew excited. "Maybe someone is bringing Pacie home."

Irma and Oscar rushed to the main door facing the driveway and opened it.

"It's Johnny," Irma said, waving at him as he walked up to them. "Pacie's not with you?"

"I was hoping she was here. Apparently, she's not." A look of concern covered Johnny's face as he walked into the foyer. Then he stared at Oscar. "What happened to your face?"

"Uh, nothing to worry about. It's just one of the chemicals in the formula I made to take out the mutants."

Oscar reached into a pocket and pulled out a tube of cream. "Irma gave me this anti-itch crap because it itches like hell."

"Glad I'm not you," Johnny said with a smile.

Oscar gathered up his beekeeper's suit and Kevlar wrappings and stuffed them into a trash bag. "I'd like to stay and chat, but I need to collect the hive and get the hornets to the shop before they wake up."

Johnny looked alarmed. "Hornets?"

"Relax, they're knocked out right now," Oscar said. "I could use your help collecting everything and getting it back to the shop, if you don't mind."

"Sure, I can help, but I don't want to miss Pacie if she shows up."

"I'm staying here. I'll call by landline if she shows up," Irma said.

"Have you searched the whole house? She could be unconscious somewhere."

"She's not here, but I'll keep looking," Irma said.

"Do you know if someone picked her up? Her car is in the driveway."

"I don't know, but it looks like she was going to ride her bike somewhere, but a tire is flat. I think she walked to wherever she went."

"If she walked, she couldn't have gone far," Johnny said. "Did she leave a note?"

"I didn't see one," Irma said. "But don't worry, I want to find her as bad as you do."

"This way." Oscar motioned for Johnny to follow him outside. He placed the bagged clothing into his van, and then he and Johnny walked over to the nest.

Irma and Mr. Dibble walked into the grand room and up to the tall windows. Irma watched him and Johnny bag up pieces of the destroyed hive.

Johnny opened the cellar door and entered the basement while Oscar gathered the rest of the nest.

Irma and Mr. Dibble rushed down to the basement and over to the men. "Is this all you have to do before you leave?"

"Yep, and we'd better be moving along," Oscar said. He stopped and looked at Irma. "Are you sure you want to stay here alone?"

"I'm not alone; I have Mr. Dibble to protect me."

Johnny picked up a bag. "I'll call and check on you later."

"By landline," Oscar chimed in. "And keep everything closed because the queen is still out there, and there could be more hornets roaming around."

"Yes, sir." Irma saluted.

After the men left by the cellar door, she made sure it was securely closed but could not figure out how to lock it. As she looked throughout the basement, she did not find Pacie, but she did find her cellphone lying on the floor. Irma placed it in her fanny pack. "Pacie's out there without her phone."

When she got back upstairs, she heard two car doors close. "What did they forget?"

She looked out the dining-room window and saw two men dressed in black walk from a black SUV and around the mansion to where Oscar and Johnny had just left. One carried a cage similar to Oscar's.

At first, she thought she should go outside and ask them what they were doing, but when she saw a handgun strapped to the hip of one of the men, she thought she had better not confront them.

Irma walked quietly to both the east and west entry doors and locked them. With stealth, she went into the grand room to see what they were doing on that side of the house.

She stood to the side of the window where she had been watching Oscar and Johnny. She occasionally peeked around the window frame to see what they were doing. It was as though they had come to see the nest, but how would they even know it was there?

"Some yahoo took it," one man said, his voice muffled through the glass.

"Are you sure this is where it was?"

"One hundred percent sure. Besides, look at the ground and the pieces left behind."

"Did they take the stingers, too?"

There was a pause, then the other one said, "They must've taken them with the hive. But the queen is still out there somewhere, according to her transceiver."

"Where, damn it!"

"She's moving and heading toward the other side of town."

"It's obvious we won't be able to collect them before the drop. There's only thirty minutes left, and we need to get out of here. We'll send the hazmat team in to recover the stingers before sunrise."

Irma looked out the window and saw them walking back to the driveway. Mr. Dibble was growling. "Shush. We don't need them to hear you and come inside looking for us."

Mr. Dibble began barking. Irma tried to quiet him as she looked back out the window. The men had stopped, discussed something, and walked back to the cellar door.

"Oh my god, they're coming inside. What do we do?"

Then she remembered Pacie showing her a hidden room in the study, behind a bookcase. She rushed to the office, hoping the men could not hear her footsteps. When she and Mr. Dibble entered the room, the only thing she could remember was which bookcase it was. She could not remember how to open it.

Irma was so nervous she could not think, but at least Mr. Dibble was not barking anymore. She pushed and pulled on the shelves, tilted books back and forth, and then she remembered; the nearby wall sconce was the unlocking mechanism. She reached up to the crystal pendant hanging below the single candle slip and pulled down on it. With a click, one side of the bookcase popped open a few inches. Then she heard the basement door underneath the central staircase open and close.

Irma pulled the secret doorway open enough for her and Mr. Dibble to slip inside. Then, with only a barely audible creek, she swung it closed until she heard the click.

In the dark, Irma kneeled and pulled Mr. Dibble close to her, ready to hold his mouth closed if she had to. At the moment, Mr. Dibble seemed to know what they were doing and remained silent.

"Whoever is in here must be hiding," one man said. His voice grew louder as they entered the study. "When I find them, I'll take pleasure in forcing them to tell me what they did with the stingers."

"We don't have much time," the gruff voiced man said. "Are they responding at all?"

There was a pause, then the other man said, "No, I'm having difficulty getting much of a signal from any of them. The enhanced blocking mechanism must be interfering with the signal. And if the queen's signal is correct, we don't have time to go to the other side of town and collect her."

"At least we still have the prototype," the gruff man said. "The dead ones we collect later after the drop will give us the information we need."

Irma heard boot heals walk toward her side of the room. The other man said, "This is a fascinating old mansion. I'll bet there's a secret passage in here."

The sound of books moving on a nearby bookshelf made Mr. Dibble put out a low growl.

"It doesn't matter. If they're hiding, they'll be dead soon."

A short alarm sounded. "We gotta go. There's only fifteen minutes before the drop."

Irma heard them leave the room. She had not triggered the light in the small hidden room, but she knew there was a peephole with a cover somewhere on the back of the bookcase. She stood up and felt the wood panel until she found the cover. She looked through the peephole and saw no one. She would have stayed in hiding for a long time, but the troubling words that whoever was hiding would soon be dead made her want to leave the secret place.

She felt around for the wall sconce on the inside and pulled on the pendant; the door swung open.

Panicked, Irma ran to the phone and called Oscar's shop, but no one answered. She left a message on the answering machine telling him about a drop and everyone dying in fifteen minutes.

Irma was so frightened she could not think. If she could find Pacie's spare keys, she would take the SUV instead of the Mustang to Oscar's because it had to be easier to drive than the manual transmission.

With haste, she looked through the desk and could not find the keys. She would have to drive the Mustang. If she was going to die, she did not want to die alone.

31

Box

Something thumped around inside the black metal box.

"There's a hornet in there," Pacie said, still struggling to free her hands.

The angry trucker looked at Pacie. "I can't believe I've been brought to the same room as you."

Pacie watched Greg squirm on the floor and wanted to say something back to him, but instead she looked at Kevin. "We have to get out of these restraints and stop them."

"I have a knife. It's in my right front pocket," Greg said. He was so angry that Pacie thought if he was not restrained he would likely punch someone. "Come on you fools, get it out."

"I'll try to get it," Pacie said. She scooted next to him and turned so that her hands could reach inside his pocket. "Stop moving or I'm not going to be able to get it out."

Pacie slid a restrained hand into his pocket. Down at the bottom, among coins, was the knife. It kept slipping through her fingers, but she finally could grasp it and pull it out.

"How does it open?" Pacie asked.

Enraged, Greg pulled himself to a sitting position. "Here, let's get back-to-back and I'll take it from you and open it."

Pacie moved next to him until she felt his hand grab hers. Greg took the folding knife, dropped it, retrieved it, and then open the blade.

"Cut the tape on my hands and then I'll cut yours." Pacie tried to pull her wrists apart.

"Don't go crying if I accidentally cut you," Greg said. "I can't see what I'm doing."

As the clock ticked on the box, Greg cut through the duct tape on Pacie's wrists, nicking her only once.

"Hurry," Gary said, that box is going to open any second.

Pacie turned and swiftly cut through Greg's tape on his wrists just as the ticking stopped. And just like a Jack-in-the-box, the lid opened, and a stinger flew out.

"It's out!" Kevin shouted. "Hurry, free me."

Pacie cut through the tape around Greg's ankles as he tried to take the knife away from her. Then she rushed over to Kevin as the hornet flew around the room, as if deciding who to sting first.

"Hurry, cut my hands free," Gary said.

Greg stood up and walked behind Pacie as if he was using her as a shield.

Pacie looked at her watch. "Ten minutes. We only have ten minutes to figure this out."

Greg ran to the door. "It's locked."

Kevin looked at the app on his phone while Pacie sprinted to the broadcasting equipment that the men had been using.

"The screen shows there's nine minutes left, but I need a code to change it. Can anyone figure this out?" Pacie wanted to tap in some random numbers, but she did not want the program to lock them out.

Kevin walked over to Pacie. "I just need to tap into the video recording for this room and see if it shows what code they punched in."

Gary bent over and rubbed his sore knee. "That's a real long shot."

"It's the only shot we have," Kevin said.

Gary watched Greg kick repeatedly at the door. The banging caught the hornet's attention. It swooped down at Greg and plunged its inches long stinger into his neck. Greg froze for a moment and dropped backward like a bag of potatoes.

"That guy just got stung," Gary said, watching Greg struggle to breathe as the hornet flew around the room.

Pacie rushed to Greg's side. As Greg's throat tightened, he squeaked out that he was allergic to bees. She immediately took her only EpiPen from her purse, pulled off the blue safety cap, and jabbed the orange end into his thigh, right through the jeans of this unpleasant man.

Pacie could not stop shaking. She knew that if the hornet stung her next, she would die and good ol' trucker Greg would be alive.

Greg's breathing eased. Pacie was standing when Greg grabbed her hand. He whispered, "Thank you."

Pacie was taken aback for a moment, not expecting those words to come out of Greg's mouth. She smiled and, upon giving a nod of you're welcome, stood and joined the others at the radio.

"Gary, I don't have my phone. Can you call 9-1-1?" Pacie pointed toward Greg. "We got to get him to the hospital."

"It's not working," Gary said, keeping an eye on the hornet's location. "We have to do something about that hornet flying around the room. It needs to be put back in that box."

"Maybe we can lure it inside," Pacie said.

Gary reached into his breast pocket and took out a snack sized candy bar. "I know they like meat, but since I don't want to be the bait, this might work."

Pacie watched Gary drop the chocolate into the black metal box and pick it up.

"Here, you crazy bastard insect," Gary said, limping toward the hornet that had perched on the top of a filing cabinet. He had one hand on the bottom of the box and the other on the back of the lid, ready to close it the moment the hornet took the bait. "I sure hope you have a sweet tooth."

Pacie wanted to yell at Gary to stop walking toward the hornet, but she was afraid it would distract it from eyeing the candy in the box.

Kevin stared at his phone. "Guys, I have good news and bad news. The good news is that I found the clip where a guy is putting in the code."

"What's the bad news?" Pacie asked.

"We only have five minutes to figure it out and stop the countdown."

"Start figuring it out." Pacie felt like screaming. "It's probably going to give you only three or four tries to get it right."

Kevin's hands shook as he tapped in what he thought was the correct sequence of numbers, but he was wrong.

Pacie could not stand the suspense. She watched Gary inch closer to the stinger. Then to her surprise, it actually took the bait. Gary immediately closed the box and fought the hornet as it thrust its body against the inside.

"This thing's strong. I'm not going to be able to hold it," Gary said as he kept the lid pressed down.

"Stand on it," Pacie blurted out. She looked around for something strong enough to put the box inside to keep the hornet contained when it escaped, but there was nothing. Then she saw a long phone charging cable that was plugged into the wall. She took the cord and wrapped it around the box, working between Gary's hands and tied a knot that would not stay tied.

"Good try," Gary said, "but that's not going to last long. And my elbow's killing me."

Pacie took the duct tape that was used to tie them up and wrapped it around the box until the roll was empty. "There, that'll hold a little while."

Gary cautiously loosened his grip. "It's holding. But I'm putting it inside the file cabinet and hope we're out of here before it escapes."

Pacie looked over at Greg, who was now sitting up and leaning against the wall by the door. Then she looked at Kevin when he slammed a fist on the table.

"I've got only one more try for the password and one more minute before we're . . ." Kevin did not finish the sentence.

Pacie and Gary ran up to him.

"You can do it," Pacie said, trying to sound encouraging.

"We trapped the bee, so don't worry about that," Gary said.

Pacie watched the video of the keypad entries. She started to speak some numbers when Kevin shushed her.

"You're confusing me," Kevin said.

Pacie was as nervous as Kevin. She brought her hands to her face as Kevin tapped the first key.

"There's only thirty seconds left," Pacie said softly.

"I know, I know."

Kevin's hand shook as he tapped the rest of the numbers and stared at the screen. "It took it. It took it."

"Stop the countdown." Pacie's heart raced.

Five. Four. Three. Two. It stopped at two.

"I think I just stopped it," Kevin said. "I think I'm going to faint."

Pacie looked at the screen to double-check that the countdown had really stopped. "Gary, can you try 9-1-1, again?"

Gary tried the call. "It's still isn't going through."

Pacie began to nervously pace the room. "I need to get help for Greg and report all this to the media before the bad guys stop us."

"Just when I was about to cheer." Kevin leaned back into the screen. "Now to stop whatever is blocking communications."

"I'll get you a stool," Pacie said, "but don't lollygag because I'm sure they'll be coming back here unless we're able to alert the police."

32

Pheromone

Traffic was not bad as Irma drove to Oscar's Vermin Control. She looked over at Mr. Dibble, sitting in the seat beside her. "People must've decided to drive back home rather than leave town."

Irma pushed in the clutch and shifted down to second as she neared a congested area. "I think I'm even getting the hang of shifting."

She looked at her watch. "Only seven minutes left? I've got to get to Oscar's before it's too late, and I die alone on this dreadful road."

A scattering of streetlamps flickered as if the power was about to go out, making the area unusually eerie. She put her lights on bright and shifted into third. She had to get to Oscar's fast.

With three minutes to spare, Irma pulled into Oscar's driveway and parked next to his van. Straight ahead, flashlights were shining on an old apple tree where Oscar and Johnny were messing with something on a limb.

Irma ran up to them. "We're all gonna be dead in a few minutes. We should get inside."

"What?" Johnny said, holding a cage for Oscar.

"I heard them, the men who want to kill us," Irma said, watching Oscar place a giant birdlike hornet into a cage.

"It's a queen," Oscar said, not immediately responding to Irma's comments. "This brand of pheromone traps works great."

"Let's put it in your van with the others," Johnny said. "Hope you don't have to drive anywhere soon."

33

The Fall

"I got it," Kevin said, wiping perspiration from his forehead. "Try your cellphone and see if you can get through to someone. I'm calling the police."

"I'll call for an ambulance," Gary said.

"Wait," Kevin said, looking at the video on his phone. "Those guys are coming back into the building. I can't believe they're able to unlock the doors. Only security has the keys."

"Forget the ambulance; we'll take Greg to the hospital ourselves," Pacie said, wishing she had not dropped her phone at the house.

"We gotta leave now." Kevin turned off the computer screen.

Gary and Kevin helped Greg stand and literally carried him down the hallway with his arms over their shoulders.

"This way," Kevin said, turning down an interior hallway. "There's a freight elevator down here. I doubt they'll be using it."

The four of them piled into the elevator. Kevin punched the first-floor button.

"This way." Kevin motioned for them to the back of the college. "There's a dock we can go out. My car's parked out there."

Pacie followed the guys as they lugged Greg, who was too weak to stand on his own. They ran past pallets of boxes and through the receiving door next to the docking bay. Kevin led them into the parking lot where his pickup truck sat.

"Four of us can't fit in the cab," Pacie said.

"This half comatose trucker guy and I will lay in the truck's bed," Gary said.

Kevin helped Gary and Greg into the back and spread out a small tarp for them to lie on.

"Let's get out of here," Pacie said, climbing into the passenger seat.

Kevin sped out of staff parking and onto the side road, heading to Black Water Hospital.

Pacie used Kevin's phone to call Irma. "Thank god you're all right."

"Where are you?" Irma asked. "I've been worried silly."

"We're on the way to the hospital," Pacie said. "Where are you?"

"I'm at Oscar's. Johnny's here, too. Oscar managed to catch a bunch of hornets, even the queen."

"Auntie Bee?"

"She would be the one."

"We'll head over there shortly. Don't go anywhere."

Pacie looked out the back window. The blue tarp flapped around the two men who looked like corpses that they had been picked up from alongside the road.

Pacie looked over at Kevin. "Did you call the police?"

"I called while we lugged that trucker around but was put on hold. I'll bet they're kinda busy."

Pacie called WBLA, the local TV station she routinely called to give updates to. After several rings, it was answered.

"WBLA."

"Janet, is that you?"

"Pacie? What's been going on?"

"What I'm going to tell you I want sent out as an emergency broadcast. I want everyone to hear it."

"No problem. Give me just a moment and I'll put you live." Moments later Janet said, "Please stand by for an important emergency message from local investigator, Pacie Rose."

While Pacie explained everything she knew and everything she suspected of the criminals and their plan to harm the residents of Black Water, Kevin's pickup bounced along on a worn-out suspension.

When Pacie finished speaking, Janet said, "That sounds so crazy, but I believe it."

"Believe it. It's true."

"I'll have it transcribed stat and put it out over the wire."

"Make sure the paper gets a copy, too."

"I will," Janet said. "Are you safe?"

"Safe enough," Pacie said. "I gotta go."

When they reached the hospital, Kevin drove around to the emergency department. The four of them went inside to a packed waiting room. All the chairs were filled and people were setting on the floor, wheezing and coughing.

"Gary, can you stay with Greg? I need Kevin to take me to Oscar's," Pacie said.

"Sure, no problem," Gary said. "I'll have them take a look at my knee and elbow while I'm here. I took a terrible spill."

"Thank you. Keep me informed, but you'll need to call Kevin's phone for now." Pacie wanted to know more about what happened to Gary, but she had to get over to Oscar's.

Kevin tried to drive like a bat out of hell to Oscar's, but many abandoned cars slowed him down before he could floor it.

"Those people can probably track the hornets to Oscar's," Pacie said.

"Don't tell me there are stingers over there where we're going."

"There is, but don't worry because they're caged, or something."

"Or something?" Kevin groaned. "If you want my advice, we should stay away from where those stingers are. I really don't want to come into contact with those thugs again."

Pacie had not fully thought it out, but being anywhere where hornets and thugs would soon congregate was asking for trouble.

Kevin almost drove by Oscar's Vermin Control. He slammed on the brakes then drove onto to the grass and parked so that he could make a clean getaway if the goons showed up.

Pacie jumped out of the pickup and ran up to Johnny who was walking out of the shop. They embraced and kissed, and kissed and embraced.

"Knock it off, you two," Oscar said. "There'll be time for that stuff later."

"We heard the emergency broadcast," Irma said, holding up her phone.

"Janet can work miracles," Pacie said. Then she introduced Kevin to the others. She looked around. "Where are the hornets?"

"They're in my van safe and sound," Oscar said. "But I think they're waking up. I can hear noises coming from the inside."

"We should get out of here before the bad guys get here," Pacie said. "I think they want to collect all the evidence relating to their clandestine war project."

"They do." Irma said. "But now that the cat's out of the bag, maybe they'll just go away."

The knocks and bangs inside the van were getting louder.

Johnny shined a light on the van. "Oscar, did you know your passenger window is down a notch?"

"Oh shit," Oscar said, about to run to the van, but stopped himself. "Those mutants can squeeze through cracks like a tricky little mouse. We'd better get into the house, and fast."

"But they're all caged or stuck in a trap," Johnny said, keeping his light focused on the van window.

There was another loud bang, like someone had pounded the side of Oscar's van with a sledgehammer.

"Those things are strong," Oscar said, wiping his nose.

Irma screamed. "Look, a hornet is squeezing through the window opening."

"That's the queen," Oscar said. "Run!"

They ran as fast as they could to Oscar's house, next to the shop. Pacie looked back just in time to see the massive queen squeeze through the crack and fly directly toward her.

Pacie made eye contact with Auntie Bee as Johnny tried to shield her, but it was no good. The queen stung Pacie in the neck. She stumbled and fell to the ground while Auntie Bee flew over to give Oscar her next kiss in the neck.

34

Destruction

Oscar burst through the front door, where Sadie was waiting to greet him. The queen was inches away from penetrating Oscar's neck when Sadie jumped up and grabbed it with her mouth. She began shaking and chomping down on it as if it were a groundhog she had caught out by the shed.

Mr. Dibble entered the house behind Irma and stopped and watched Sadie as if waiting for her to share her new toy.

"Did it sting you?" Kevin asked Oscar as he held the door open for the others.

Oscar reached for his neck. "No, I don't think so."

Johnny carried Pacie inside and laid her on the couch. She struggled to breathe while he rummaged through her satchel looking for the EpiPen she always carried. "Her EpiPen isn't in here. She'll die if she doesn't get the shot."

"She used it on the trucker," Kevin said. "She saved his life."

"And lost her own." Johnny was angry as he repositioned her head to what he thought would help her breathe, but she still gasped for air as the wheezing grew louder.

"I'm calling 9-1-1," Kevin said pulling the phone from his pants pocket. "What's the address here?"

Oscar took a letter from the kitchen counter and shoved it into Keven's hand, and pointed. "Right there."

Irma kneeled at Pacie's head; tears welled up in her eyes. "Hang in there, Pacie. Help is on the way."

"It's just like her to give her only shot to someone in need." Johnny shook his head as his jaw muscles tightened.

"Her airway is closing." Irma began to hyperventilate as a panic attack set in. "Somebody, do something."

Pacie wheezed as she tried to pull in air through a swollen and constricted airway. All her energy was focused on breathing.

Oscar ran into the bathroom. Sounds of items being thrown around made it clear he was searching for something.

"I got it!" Oscar shouted as he ran back into the living room. "This generic epinephrine is old, and probably expired, but it should work."

Johnny grabbed it from him and jabbed it into Pacie's thigh muscle.

Everyone stood silent as Pacie's breathing was about to cease; she could not pull any more air into her lungs.

"She's dead!" Irma wailed.

As if what they were looking at was a dream, not to be responded to, Pacie suddenly gulped in air. She took in a labored breath and then another.

"Pacie, you're alive," Irma said between sobs.

"Damned right she's alive," Johnny said. "Where's that ambulance? You called, right?" He looked at Kevin who was trembling as if standing in a grocery store freezer.

"I did. I did," Kevin said. "They said they'd send an ambulance."

Oscar looked at Sadie, who had dropped the queen on the dining room floor and began growling. She stepped back with Mr. Dibble as a piercing beep emanated from the mutant hornet.

"What the hell?" Oscar said, pulling Sadie further away from Auntie Bee just as it exploded, spewing bits and pieces of flesh, hair, feathers, and guts several feet into the air.

Everyone screamed, or at least jumped with fright from the shock of the explosion.

"What happened?" Pacie squeaked out.

"She talked." Irma jumped for joy.

"That bee self-destructed," Kevin said.

Pacie smiled. "Auntie Bee is dead?"

"You got it, girl," Johnny said, pulling strands of perspiration soaked hair from her forehead. "Don't talk. Just breathe."

"Your nemesis is indeed dead," Irma said.

Pacie looked at Johnny. "You're crying."

Johnny blinked his eyes. "I'm not crying. I'm just. . . happy you're . . ."

Pacie reached up and wiped a tear from his cheek. "I love you."

"It was Oscar who saved you," Johnny said, holding her hand. "He had a dose of that bee venom stuff."

"It was my dear, late Eleanor's medicine," Oscar said, solemnly. "I'm glad I never threw it away. I didn't even throw away her ol' stained rooster apron; it's still hanging in the pantry."

"I hear sirens," Kevin said, glancing toward a darkened window.

"You must have good ears, young man," Oscar said, looking at the bits and pieces of the queen. "I'd better get this cleaned up before the paramedics run a stretcher through it and spread the mutant mess all over the place."

"I'll help you," Kevin said, following Oscar to the pantry. He took the zipper storage bags Oscar handed him.

"I want to keep all the body parts and mechanical things you find," Oscar told Kevin.

Oscar and Kevin had a path cleared in the dining room when the ambulance arrived. The paramedics put Pacie on the stretcher and took her out to the transport vehicle.

"I'm following you to the hospital," Irma told Johnny as he climbed into the back of the ambulance with Pacie. "I'll leave Mr. Dibble here with Sadie."

When Oscar and Kevin finished collecting Auntie Bee's flesh, Oscar took the bags out to the shop and put them in the freezer.

"I can't believe you're saving all this sick stuff?" Kevin said, walking to the sink.

"Gary and I have a lot of studying to do on the parts," Oscar said as he washed his hands in the shop's utility basin. When finished, he went into the store and noticed the printouts of the hornet he took from Pacie's mansion in the printer's output tray. He picked up the pictures. "I'll be damned. I forgot I had a souvenir of those mutants and proof they really existed."

"Oh, crap," Kevin said, moving in close to get a look at the images. "You'd better put that in a safe or something,"

Oscar put the pictures between the pages of a chemical supply catalog. "That's good enough for now. They'll get moved again when the shop's taken away."

"You're not making enough money to keep it?"

Oscar shrugged. "Could be doing better."

"Sorry to hear that." Kevin looked at Oscar's flushed face. "Don't take this the wrong way, but is your face always that red? Is it from high blood pressure or stress or something?"

"No, my face isn't always this red." Oscar grumbled as he switched off the shop light.

Kevin said nothing and followed Oscar out to his van.

"When I'm done moving these freaks, I'm going to head to the hospital. You can come with me if you want." Oscar opened the van door. "You've got to be kidding. These hornets exploded, too. There's a mess all over the place."

Kevin looked at the slime that coated the inside of Oscar's van. "You can ride with me."

PART V

The Gathering

35

Oz

Doctor Plum removed his stethoscope from Pacie's chest. "Sounds good. I'll discharge you home today."

"Thank you, Doctor," Pacie said. She looked at the bright streaks of sunlight that streamed between the slats of the hospital room's window shade and onto the white bedspread.

Doctor Plum hung the stethoscope around his neck and put his hands in the pockets of his unbuttoned lab coat that draped around his pudgy body. "Do you have any questions?"

"Can you write me a prescription for some EpiPens?"

"Consider it done," the doctor said. He walked toward the door, stopped, and turned around. "I want to thank you for saving our town and our people. And I can tell from all the visitors you have in your room, I'm not alone."

"Thank you, Doctor. But it was a group effort. Lots of people had a part to play."

Doctor Plum nodded and left the room.

Pacie looked at Johnny, who was sitting in a chair next to the bed. "I get to go home."

"I'm happy for you," Johnny said, holding her hand. "You can stay with me while you recover."

Amanda, standing next to her husband, quickly added, "Or you can stay with us, Mom. You know we have an extra bedroom."

"I bet Grandma wants to be alone," Charlotte said as a matter of fact. "I know how she thinks."

"Char wins," Pacie said. "I feel fine. And I'm looking forward to my own bed . . . and food."

"Well," Irma said. "I'm going to be checking in on you and seeing how you're doing."

Pacie smiled. "That's okay. I can't argue with you anyway."

Irma's phone rang. "Bart, I'm happy you called. . . . I'm at the hospital visiting Pacie. . . . She goes home today. . . . I'd like that. See you soon."

"What's going on?" Pacie asked.

Irma beamed. "Bart's going to have Tara drop him off here and he'll ride back to the marina with me."

"Cousin Irma has a boyfriend," Char said playfully.

Pacie looked over at Oscar and Kevin, who were leaning against the windowsill. "Oscar, thank you again for saving my life."

"Aw, shucks," Oscar's face grew redder. "It was just my sentimental self not being able to throw my dear Eleanor's things away."

"Sentimental?" Kevin grinned.

"Yes, sentimental," Oscar scoffed. "You don't know me, young man. I can, on occasion, be sentimental."

Everyone laughed.

Gary hobbled into the room, trying to manage his new crutches. Greg tagged behind him. "Glad I didn't miss the party. How are you doing?"

"Good to see you, Gary. I get to go home today. How about you?"

"They wrapped my knee and gave me some pain medicine," Gary said. "I'm supposed to stay off the knee for a while. So now I can catch up on my TV programs."

"That sounds like a plan," Pacie said. She looked at Greg, who was moving up to her. Then she glanced at Irma, who was frowning.

Greg cleared his throat. "Thank you for giving me your only epinephrin shot and saving my life."

Pacie smiled and nodded. "You're welcome."

Greg looked uneasy as he looked around the crowded room. "And I want to apologize for the way I treated you and your friend—"

"Cousin," Irma interrupted.

Greg looked at Irma and then back down toward the floor. "And you're not an old biddy."

"You'd better quit while you're ahead, kid," Oscar said.

"I'm sorry," Greg said, backing to the side of the room.

"It's all right," Pacie said. She was too happy to be angry with the once obnoxious trucker. "It's water under the bridge now."

The room was quiet until Mr. and Mrs. Handy walked in with their helper, Dale.

"Where's the booze?" Mr. Handy said as he pulled a blue tartan handkerchief from a back of his bib overalls. "It's a party in here."

"If it was the old days, I'd have a bottle stashed in the bottom drawer of this nightstand." Pacie laughed, then looked at Dale. "How are you, Dale? Must be you're going home."

"I am, Ms. Rose," Dale said, softly. "At first, they didn't think I was going to make it because I got stung so many times."

"I'm glad you're okay now."

"I'm giving the boy some time off to recover." Mr. Handy blew his nose. "Did you hear how long those stingers were?"

"They were long, to be sure," Pacie said.

Mrs. Handy smoothed the front of her paisley dress. "We got an email that local beekeepers are going to donate hives to the orchard to make up for all the ones we lost because of. . . whatever those things were."

"That's good news," Pacie said. "Sounds like things are getting back to normal."

"Listen to this," Irma said, looking at her phone. "I'm going to turn up the volume."

A male voice from the phone's speaker said, "I repeat, the secret operation known as Dark Knight has been stopped. The top secret weapons of war developed by an illicit segment of the Department of Defense have been neutralized. Intelligence agents have been apprehended and are now in the custody of the state police. Stay tuned for further updates."

"We could all be dead right now," Kevin said as he paced in front of the room's window.

"But we're not," Oscar said. "I for one am going to sleep with one eye open."

Then Mayor Castleman entered the room with the crew of the WBLA television news team right behind him.

"Can this room get any more crowded?" Mr. Castleman boisterously said, walking up to Pacie. "I hope you don't mind that I brought Miss Janet and Carlos along. I want the citizens of Black Water to know that everything is under control and there is no need to worry."

Pacie saw Janet with a microphone in her hand and Carlos point the camera at her. It was not as though she had much of a choice. "Sure, it's fine."

"With your consent," Mr. Castleman said as he handed Pacie a framed certificate. "I'd like to present you, Ms. Pacie Rose, hero of our beloved town of Black Water, a certificate of valor for going above and beyond the call of duty; and exhibiting exceptional courage, extraordinary decisiveness and presence of mind along with unusual swiftness of action, regardless of your personal safety to save or protect human life."

Pacie was not expecting such an honor. She thanked the mayor and smiled at the camera as she took the certificate. "It was a group effort, to be sure."

"I'm not done," Mr. Castleman said as though he was the Wizard of Oz. He moved to Oscar. "My dear man, Mr. Oscar Schattschneider, savior of the peacemaker and tamer of beasts, I'd like to present to you a check for ten-thousand American dollars and a very lucrative contract for the purchase of your pesticide that tamed the weapons of destruction without killing them. Would you like to accept this offer?"

Oscar was speechless as he rubbed his sleeveless arm in thought. Then he took the check and the contract that the mayor handed him. "I'll need to give this contract a good lookin' over before I sign on the dotted line."

"You'll be able to fix your van and update the shop," Gary said. "Your hard work literally paid off."

"Yes, Gary, I think you're right," Oscar said, studying the check.

There was a knock at the door, then a nurse in green scrubs entered the room. "I hate to break up the celebration, but Dr. Plum is discharging Pacie and I need to go over the discharge instructions with her."

Everyone, except Johnny and Irma, said their goodbyes and left the room.

"You're quite the hero," the nurse said as she sat on the other side of the bed.

"It is quite humbling."

The nurse smiled. "Let's goes through this and get you out of here."

As the nurse finished discharging Pacie, Bart walked into the room. With his usual gravelly voice, he said, "Oh, I'm sorry. The door was open."

"You're fine, Bart," Pacie said, taking the prescription the nurse handed her. "Come on in."

Bart gave a nod to the nurse as she left the room. "Must be you're feeling better and going home."

"I'm back to normal and can't wait to . . . blow this joint, as they say."

Johnny laughed. "You must be feeling better."

Pacie watched Bart and Irma meet in the center of the room. He held her hand and planted a kiss on Irma's cheek.

"I hope I just wasn't too forward, Irma," Bart said, waiting for her response. "I'm relieved nothing happened to you."

Irma blushed. "Not at all, Bartholomew. Not at all."

* * *

Pacie leaned into Johnny on the deck seat of the Zombie Refuge sailing yacht anchored down far offshore of Black Water. The gentle breeze was perfectly warm and the sky a robin's egg blue. Cumulus clouds lined up on the far west horizon, too far away to worry about, yet held the promise of a beautiful sunset to come.

"What's in that picnic basket of yours?" Johnny asked.

"Homemade peach cobbler for one," Pacie said. "Do you want some?"

"Not now. We'd better focus on fishing." Johnny said, looking at their short rod and real setup on the stanchion of the boat. "We haven't caught the main dish yet."

"Are you sure you know how to fish?" Pacie teased. "Maybe we're supposed to be moving a little."

Johnny tickled her in the ribs. "I might not be an expert, but at least I try."

"Oh, look," Pacie said, standing. "I think I caught something."

"Can you pull it in?" Johnny asked, watching the pole bob up and down. "Wind it in slowly."

"I'm gonna try."

Johnny watched as Pacie pulled in a small silvery salmon. "You caught a Chinook but unfortunately I don't think that's a keeper. It's too small."

"I've caught more fish than you," Pacie said, watching Johnny take it off the hook and toss it back into the water. "So I guess I win."

"I don't think there's much winning because there's nothing to eat."

"What do you mean there's nothing to eat?" Pacie said with good cheer. "There's my peach cobbler."

"I guess I can choke that down," Johnny said playfully.

"Well, it can't be any worse than your sailing skills," Pacie said. "Which are literally nonexistent. Are you sure Bart gave you lessons?"

"I got us out on the water, didn't I?"

"The boat's motor got us out here." Pacie laughed.

"Okay then, what now?" Johnny said. "I'm starving."

"Let's just enjoy the day with no giant hornets roaming around," Pacie said.

Johnny pulled Pacie close and was about to kiss her when a buzzing sound caught his attention.

Pacie watched as a normal-sized hornet circled them and then flew off.

They looked at each other with relief and began laughing.

"I'm gonna be super paranoid of bees for a long, long time," Pacie said.

"You and me both, babe. You and me both."

The End

* * *

Thank you for reading!

ConnieMyres.com

DID YOU MISS THE FIRST BOOK IN THE SERIES?

SLENDERMAN: PACIE ROSE MYSTERIES, #1

When children disappear and citizens are murdered in a Lake Michigan resort town, will a citizen reporter and her quirky sidekick cousin be able to stop what witnesses describe as a faceless, tall skinny man in a black suit before grief and death touch everyone in town?

Citizen reporter Pacie Rose is in her strawberry with her family when Irma, her offbeat sidekick cousin, calls and reports that there's been a child abduction in town. They take on the self-appointed case of finding the culprit while murders and another missing child pile up. Armed with tools from the priest and local college professor, they are ready to confront the thing that witnesses describe as a tall man who wears a black suit and who appears to have no face.

The resort town of Black Water is inundated with so many weird events that Pacie Rose took up being the town's citizen reporter. With her quirky cousin as the sidekick, they work to assist authorities in solving cases. Not bound by institutional rules, they can investigate using "not so legal" ways to get information.

The Potawatomi have told of strange occurrences in the area long before the construction of the nuclear power plant in the 1960s. However, ever since Bulwark became operational, aberrations have increased substantially. Missing people, cryptids, UFOs, the paranormal, and alternate dimensions are just a few of the mysterious encounters.

Follow Pacie as she works to rid Black Water of the terrifying phenomena.

BONUS: My Name Is Mr. Dibble and Jezebel companion short stories are included.

ConnieMyres.com

ALSO BY CONNIE MYRES

STAND-ALONE BOOKS

Jezebel • My Name is Mr. Dibble • Ring • Haunting of Ender House • Rest Stop Terror • Solus • Who Killed Sweet Violet? • Lucifer's Island • Raven's Ridge

PACIE ROSE MYSTERIES

Slenderman • Hornet • Wolf

RANCOR

Rancor: A Paranormal Psychological Thriller (Books 1 & 2) Sinister Attachments • Unrestrained

SEVEN SEALS REDUX

Seven Seals Redux: The Complete Apocalyptic Novel Series (Books 1-7) White Horse • Red Horse • Black Horse • Pale Horse • Tribulation • Signs • Trumpets

SUSPENSE STORIES

Suspense Stories #1: Raven's Ridge, Lucifer's Island, Sinister Attachments (Suspense Stories, #1)

WATCH FOR SPOOKY SHORTS

A collection of creepy short stories, A-Z. Spooky Shorts A-G: A Collection of Creepy Short Stories Apple Pie • Black-Eyed Kids • Creature • Dungeon • Electric • Fairy • Genie • House • Ice • Joker • Kiss • Lucid • Minion •

*Neighbor • Obelisk • Pattern • Quest • Rumor • Squatch •
Time • Underworld • Visitor • Wolf • X-axis • Yellow • ZoZo.*

* * *

The complete list can be found at ConnieMyres.com

ABOUT THE AUTHOR

CONNIE MYRES writes books and short stories in the horror, mystery, suspense, and science fiction genres. She is an author, developer, and registered nurse. Sometime in the future—whether by choice or by arm-twisting—she will join the digital nomad movement.

Born and raised in Michigan, she has been creating stories since childhood. Children she had babysat as a teenager loved to hear her mystery stories, especially since she carefully included all the children listening into the storyline, causing suspense for everyone.

Connie's website: https://www.ConnieMyres.com

FEATHER AND FERMION PUBLISHING

Founded in 2014, Feather and Fermion Publishing proudly publishes horror, mystery, suspense, thriller, science fiction and fantasy stories. Our imprints—Oort Cloud Books and White-Knuckle Books—publish original fiction with the mission to entertain readers.

Author Connie Myres owns Feather and Fermion Publishing.

Visit Connie's Website

Visit Connie's website and find her blog, books,, podcast, and where you can follow her on social media.

ConnieMyres.com

PEACH COBBLER

Pacie made this recipe for the fishing trip.

INGREDIENTS

4 cups peeled and sliced fresh peaches

1 cup granulated sugar

1 tablespoon cornstarch

1 teaspoon vanilla extract

1/4 teaspoon ground cinnamon

1/4 teaspoon ground nutmeg

1/4 teaspoon salt

1 cup all-purpose flour

1 cup granulated sugar

1/2 cup unsalted butter, cold and cut into small pieces

1 teaspoon baking powder

1/4 teaspoon baking soda

1/4 teaspoon salt

1/2 cup *buttermilk

INSTRUCTIONS

1. Preheat oven to 375°F (190°C).
2. In a large bowl, combine the peaches, 1 cup sugar, cornstarch, vanilla extract, cinnamon, nutmeg, and 1/4 teaspoon salt. Mix well and pour into a 9x13-inch baking dish.

3. In a separate bowl, combine the flour, 1 cup sugar, baking powder, baking soda, and 1/4 teaspoon salt. Mix well.

4. Add the butter to the flour mixture and use a pastry cutter or your fingers to cut the butter into the flour mixture until the mixture resembles coarse crumbs.

5. Stir in the buttermilk to form a dough.

6. Drop spoonfuls of the dough over the peach mixture in the baking dish.

7. Bake for 40-45 minutes, or until the top is golden brown and the filling is bubbly.

8. Serve warm with ice cream or whipped cream, if desired.

Buttermilk Substitute: For each cup of buttermilk needed, use 1 tablespoon of lemon juice or distilled white vinegar plus enough milk to measure 1 cup. Stir, then let stand for 5 minutes.

Hummingbird Food Recipe

INGREDIENTS

4 cups water

1 cup granulated white sugar

INSTRUCTIONS

1. In a large saucepan, bring the water to a boil.

2. Once the water is boiling, add the sugar and stir until it is completely dissolved.

3. Remove the saucepan from heat and allow the mixture to cool.

4. Once cooled, pour the mixture into a hummingbird feeder or a shallow dish.

5. Clean the feeder or dish every few days, and refill with fresh nectar as needed.

Note: Never use honey, brown sugar, artificial sweeteners or red food coloring